James Rochfort Maguire, Dr. Jameson

Cecil Rhodes

A Biography and Appreciation by Imperialist

James Rochfort Maguire, Dr. Jameson

Cecil Rhodes
A Biography and Appreciation by Imperialist

ISBN/EAN: 9783337099596

Printed in Europe, USA, Canada, Australia, Japan

Cover: Foto ©Raphael Reischuk / pixelio.de

More available books at **www.hansebooks.com**

CECIL RHODES.

CHAPTER I.

THE WINNING OF WEALTH.

ANYONE who had come to the Diamond Fields in Griqualand early in the seventies might have observed a tall English lad sitting at a table diamond-sorting, or superintending the work of his gang of Kaffirs, near the edge of the huge open chasm or quarry which then constituted the mines. That was the time of individual enterprise, and the rough and ready methods of surface work. A man bought a claim independently or went shares with others, roughed it in a tent, and, with the assistance of a gang of natives, got through the work himself. The

B

diamond-bearing yellow ground was beaten up and broken small by Kaffirs ; the broken yellow gravel was sifted and passed over the table at which the claim-owner sat, keen-eyed to pick out the rough gems, and swift to rake away the refuse. A primitive way of working and living it was that then obtained at Colesberg Kopje, where the town of Kimberley now stands. The diamond-seeker sat at his table in the open air, exposed to the burning Griqualand sun and the gravelly dust that rose in clouds from the sieves of the sorters. No one would have sup- posed that the future of a great Continent was bound up in the life of the dreamy, carelessly dressed English youth, who sat there daily at the diamond sorting ; and yet it was in such surroundings, that the direction in which his life-work was to be done first dawned on the mind of the Englishman, who was one day to make history, and paint the map red on a large scale, in South and Central Africa.

The younger son of a Hertfordshire clergy-

man, Cecil Rhodes came out to South Africa in
1871, and joined his elder brother Herbert,
who was engaged in cotton-growing in Natal.
The climate of Natal was the inducement
which brought the delicate youth to South
Africa. In 1872 Cecil entered at Oriel Col-
lege, Oxford, but came back to Africa the
same year, his lungs having become seriously
affected from a chill caught after rowing. Not
long after Cecil came out to Natal, his
brother Herbert was drawn away from the
slow results of cotton-planting to the dazzling
possibilities of wealth to be swiftly won near
the place now known as Kimberley. Cecil remained in Natal, but followed his brother to
Griqualand the year after. The discovery of
diamonds on the Vaal River had been followed
by the discovery of the dry diggings, in the
place where De Beers now carry on their work,
and there the future head of the Diamond
Mines found a straight way to wealth and
power.

Herbert's claim turned out well, and it was not very long before the roving disposition of the elder Rhodes led him to hand over the management to his somewhat dreamy but hard-working and persevering younger brother. Cecil had a share in his brother's claim, and ultimately took over the working, and left Herbert free to follow the more congenial life of gold-seeker, hunter, and explorer in the far North, an adventurous life, which came to an untimely end owing to the accidental burning of the hut in which he was sleeping when elephant-hunting near the Shiré. The more tenacious younger brother, Cecil, persevered at the diggings and prospered amazingly, and here it was that he became associated with Mr. C. D. Rudd, who has had so considerable a part in all his great enterprises.

Not satisfied with the hard work he did in the search for and purchase of diamonds, the immense and restless energy, which was already a characteristic of young Cecil Rhodes, found

vent in the excitement of all sorts of schemes
for making money, from a contract to pump
out a mine to the working of an ice-manufac-
turing machine, in which he and Mr. Rudd
interested themselves, for the refreshment of the
thirsty diamond diggers and the benefit of their
own pockets.   A tall, raw English youth, little
more than a sixth form schoolboy in age and
appearance, careless in his dress, abrupt, from
shyness, in his manner, young Rhodes was
already in power of brain and will far ahead of
the older men around him, and was noted for
the independence and originality of his views
of men and things.   Deep in thoughts and
schemes that reached far beyond the little world
of the Diamond fields, Cecil Rhodes, when he
came to be known, was generally regarded as
somewhat eccentric and a dreamer, though
admitted to be a far-sighted man of business,
with a head for finance.

He was often to be seen on the Diamond
fields keeping his gang of Kaffir labourers at

their work, breaking up and sifting the diamond-bearing yellow ground, while he sat on an up-turned bucket supervising them, his eyes on a book, or his mind deep in thought, out of which study and solitary thinking the dream of Empire to the North gradually emerged and took definite shape. At first, and, indeed, for a considerable time, the enjoyment of the excitement of making money kept the young diamond-digger and financier in embryo occupied; but, as time went on, he perceived that money was worth possessing for the power that it bestowed; for gold not steel was obviously the Archimedes' lever of the modern world, in which he found himself.

At exactly what period he began to be conscious of the magnetism of Africa, the attraction of that vast unexplored region to the North, which was one day to receive from him its name, he would himself find it very hard to say. But, at any rate, he had already for many years ruminated over the idea when, sixteen

years ago at Kimberley, he unbosomed himself
thus to a friend.   Moving his hand as a pointer
over the map of Africa, up to the Zambesi, he
said, " That's my dream—all English " ; a very
Utopian dream, as it must have seemed to
an unimaginative man of the world at the
time.   Yet the dream of that young English
diamond-digger was to be more important to
his adopted country, and, in due time, to his
mother country, than all the petty wars, the
elections, and the burning questions of the
day, which occupy for a moment the attention
of our passing generations.   As commonly is
the case, the judgment of his contemporaries on the man and his ideas was very
wide of the mark, and, of course, no one
guessed for a moment that the far-seeing young
financier had the destiny of South Africa in his
keeping.   Nevertheless, he was the appointed
instrument to preserve for and present to England the most permanently valuable because the
most habitable portion of the last great Conti-

nent that waited to be annexed; and his love
of the excitement of money-making, and his remarkable genius for finance, were to supply the
first of the two necessary instruments by which
the realisation of the dream of Empire to the
North might be made practicable—the instrument of money and the command of moneyed
men.

As a general rule it must be admitted that
successful money-getting tends to become mere
money-grubbing, and is the dry rot of anything great and magnanimous in a man. But
Cecil Rhodes was from the first an exception.
He never cared for money for itself, to hoard
it, or to spend it in luxury or ostentation. His
wants remained perfectly simple, and the
possession of riches did not make him change
his mode of life, or spend more upon himself.
At first he cared for money-making because he
enjoyed the excitement of success, as a marks-
man enjoys bringing down a difficult shot, or
a fox-hunter enjoys taking a stiff fence; but

gradually his financial schemes all centred round and were undertaken to advance his one dominant idea, the expansion and consolidation of Greater Britain in South Africa, the occupation for England of the seemingly illimitable and unexplored regions to the North, up to and beyond the Zambesi. This one paramount idea which had, at an early date, begun to possess the mind of young Cecil Rhodes, is certainly to be found unmistakably behind all his great financial schemes; for instance, in the change in the De Beers Trust Deed, made at the time of the amalgamation, by which the future-seeing amalgamator armed himself for his coming efforts in the North by getting for himself power to use the De Beers money and support with the wealth of the great diamond monopoly his vast schemes of Imperial Expansion in the then unfooted hinterland.

Little did his fellow-miners think, as they passed the dreamy youth with the impassive face gazing into vacancy, that the building of

an empire, the occupation of the last unoccupied Continent, was gradually assuming form
under the shaping power of that young diamond-
digger's imagination. The paramount idea in
his mind, the expansion of our Empire and its
supremacy in South Africa, was, of course, developed, and gained shape and consistency,
under the influence of the study of history and
the experience of life. This idea has been to
him through life what a great passion for a
woman is to some men, what a supreme friendship is to others. An enlightened patriotism
has gradually become the one paramount sentiment of the great South African's life; and
putting one's self in his place and looking with
his eyes on the world, one can understand his
far-reaching saying that territory is everything,
territory, that is to say, fit to support and breed
a fine race of men. He sees with his mind's
eye the vicious weaklings bred in the unsani-
tary conditions of our over-crowded English
cities, and compares them with the magnificent

race of Englishmen that might be raised on the fertile soil and in the fine air of the uplands of Rhodesia, and, as he reflects, the great need for England seems to be territory. England can supply the men in ever-increasing numbers to colonize it, but suitable land for them to colonize is strictly limited, and therefore to England such territory for her expansion is all important.

"Having read the histories of other countries," to quote Mr. Rhodes upon himself, "I saw that expansion was everything, and that the world's surface being limited, the great object of present humanity should be to take as much of the world as it possibly could." With expansion, then, as his paramount idea, and with a very definite intention of carrying out this idea in the hinterland to the North, Mr. Rhodes pushed on his big scheme of amalgamating the diamond-mines, which, owing to over-competition and over-production, were in a bad way, and over which he purposed to establish, in place of cut-throat competition, a strict monopoly. With that bull-dog tenacity and patience which are such strong notes of his character, he gradually overcame the opposition of the various interests; but it took some twenty years of steady labour and extra-ordinary skill in dealing with men to bring about the completion of his scheme, which issued in the formation of the De Beers Consolidated Mines, now the most wealthy and successfully managed mining corporation in the world. Some slight conception of the difficulties that had to be overcome, may be gained by the consideration that there were, even as late as 1885, after over one thousand properties had been amalgamated into companies, more than forty companies, as well as over fifty private properties. The De Beers Company, founded in 1880, was the centre round which the process of consolidation went on. The De Beers Company gradually acquired the other companies, till at last the De Beers Consolidated Mines had amalgamated with itself all the properties of any importance; and the Kimberley, the Dutoitspan, and Bultfontein mines, were included with the mine which gave its name to the company formed by the amalgamation. This amalgamation created a virtual monopoly, and enabled the governing mind of Mr. Rhodes to limit the output so as exactly to supply the world's demand for diamonds each year, and thus to regulate and maintain the price.

This, the first and chiefest financial work of Cecil Rhodes's life, revealed the fact that there had appeared in South Africa a business man of supreme ability, a financier without a superior — indeed, without a rival. The capitalisation of De Beers now amounts to nearer thirty than twenty-five millions, and the company pays steadily increasing dividends to the amount, at present, of about a million and a-half a year, while it watches for and buys up any new diamond-mine that might prove a dangerous rival. In this consolidation, his greatest achievement in finance, Mr. Rhodes had the co-operation of his friend, Mr. Beit, whose public spirited and powerful support has never been wanting to his friend's projects, and has helped to ensure the success of Mr. Rhodes in other undertakings, such as the obtaining of the Concession from Lobengula, which led to the formation of the Chartered Company and the after development of the Northern territory itself.

Diamonds had already given Mr. Rhodes wealth, and when the gold-mines of the Rand were discovered in 1886, he joined with his old partner in the diamond-fields, Mr. Rudd, and founded the Gold Fields of South Africa, which, after certain vicissitudes, has ultimately proved a remarkably successful trust company, having paid for the last two years dividends of 125 per cent., in addition to a large sum to the founders, who last year consented to capitalize their interest on very fair terms. Thus, both

in diamonds and in gold, Mr. Rhodes has been
associated with thoroughly sound and solid enterprises, which have gradually progressed, and
at last splendidly rewarded all who had faith
in the careful and conservative finance which
have distinguished all his undertakings.   The
success of these enterprises was to pave the way
for the yet more gigantic venture, which was to
make large demands on all the strong financial
influence, as well as the great financial reputation of its founder, I mean the greatest company of our own or any time in the matter of
colonization and development, the famous
Chartered Company of South Africa.

The great success of his own undertakings
had brought Mr. Rhodes and his friends
large fortune; but the hard-working maker
of that success was not for one moment
immersed in money-getting.   He cared for
the possession of wealth only as a means to
an end.   Money and a following of moneyed
men who had learned from experience to trust

him, were, he knew, absolutely necessary to the gigantic scheme which he had been gradually developing in his mind, the occupation of that portion of the last unoccupied Continent which seemed most fit for permanent colonization by white men.

Of course, he was well aware of the nature of the territories which now bear his name, for hunters like Selous, and explorers like Baines, had wandered over them for years and brought accurate reports of fine climate and great fertility, while the gold offered for sale by the natives, added the possibility of that rapidity of settlement and development which comes from payable gold mines alone. But while the element of financial power was necessary to the realization of Mr. Rhodes's dream of expansion, financial power, he knew, was not the only requisite. To financial power must be added political power, and it was with the intention of obtaining political power and using it to assist his great idea of expansion, that Mr. Rhodes went into politics.

When Mr. Rhodes resolved to enter upon political life he had already a better equipment of book knowledge than might have been expected. In the midst of all his diamond-digging and money-making, he had found time to read. Often he watched his natives, a book in his hand, and this study of books ended in his returning to Oriel in 1876, keeping his terms, passing his examinations, and in 1881 taking his degree. He spent the long vacation each year at work on the Diamond Fields, the rest of the year at Oxford. It is characteristic of the ambition of this much-toiling man of business, that the recreation he gave himself after laborous years of diamond-mining and finance, consisted in fresh work; where another man would have sought amusement, Mr. Rhodes sought knowledge, and when he left Oriel and Oxford he had laid a firm foundation, on which

c

he has since built, to good purpose. When one considers the difficulty of keeping the terms from South Africa, and the awkwardness to a successful man of business, who had pushed to the front in the battle of life, of coming among lads fresh from school, one realizes how strong must have been the resolve that made the successful diamond-miner and financier an Oxford undergraduate.

There are few stories of his life at this period. I remember one. About the year 1877, two Englishmen, strangers to one another, the one a middle-aged, the other a young man, occupied a post-cart on their way to Kimberley. It was before the railway was built, and they were several days together. Englishmen are naturally reserved and stiff to strangers, and between these two conversation was not promoted by the fact that the younger man kept diligently studying his prayer book. The older man's curiosity was roused, but being of a very reserved nature he said nothing.

A couple of days had passed, when, his curiosity at last overcoming his reserve, he asked the younger man what he was reading. " The Thirty-nine Articles," was the reply. This broke the ice, and the two got to know each other. The older man was Charles Warren, on his way up to make the boundary for the Free State; the younger man was the diamond-digger, Cecil Rhodes, on his way back from Oxford to Kimberley for the long vacation, and he was characteristically using his time in the post-cart, before he plunged again into the midst of diamonds and finance, in learning the Thirty-nine Articles for his next examination at Oxford.

CHAPTER II.

ABOUT fifteen years ago Cecil Rhodes entered the Cape Parliament as member for Barkly West, and came down to the Cape Assembly, as he observed in his last speech at the banquet in his honour at Cape Town, " with the thought, if possible, to use my political power to obtain the balance of unclaimed country."

Early in the eighties, at the opening of his political career, his great abilities were perceived by no less a man than General Gordon. There are very slender materials for this part of Mr. Rhodes's life shortly after he entered the Cape Assembly; but I can give some interesting, and till now unpublished, reminiscences of his intercourse with General Gordon in Basutoland. Gordon had been sent up by the Cape Government to arrange terms of peace with the Basutos. Rhodes, then the young member for Barkly West, had gone up as one of the Compensation Commission to compensate the loyal natives who had lost everything in the war, in which they had sided with the Cape Government. Gordon and Rhodes naturally came together, and used to go out long walks in company. What would not one give for a phonograph which would record those conversations? Gordon, who was a trifle dictatorial, on several occasions vigorously criticised Rhodes's independent opinions. "You always contradict me," he said, "I never met such a man for his own opinion. You think your views are always right and everyone else wrong." Rhodes was not long in getting his opportunity for retaliation. The Basutos made much of Gordon. They came in thousands to the Indabas, recognising in him a big man, and

obviously taking him for the chief man there.
"Do you know," said Rhodes to Gordon one
day, "I have an opinion that you are doing
very wrong. You are letting those Basutos
make a great mistake. They take you for the
great man, look up to you, and pay no attention
to Sauer. Whereas he is the great man here,
and you are only in his employment." Sauer
was a village attorney of Aliwal North, but was
Secretary for Native Affairs, a member of the
Cape Government by whom Gordon was employed. "You ought to explain to the Basutos
the truth that he is somebody and you are
nobody," went on Rhodes unrelentingly. This
was said chaffingly by way of a score off Gordon;
but Gordon took it quite seriously. At the
next Indaba, accordingly, Gordon stepped out
before the chiefs and, pointing to Mr. Sauer,
explained to their astonishment: "You are
making a mistake in treating me as the great
man, that is the great man of the Whites. I am
only his servant, only his dog; nothing more."

After the Indaba was over Gordon remarked to Rhodes, "I did it because it was the right thing," and then, after a pause, added, half under his breath, "but it was hard, very hard." Nevertheless, Gordon took to the young Englishman with the big ideas and independent mind, and one day, when they were out taking a walk, asked Rhodes what he was going to do after he had completed his work on the Compensation Commission. Rhodes explained that he was going home to Kimberley to look after the diamond mines. "Stay with me in Basutoland," said Gordon, "we can work together." Rhodes refused, pointing out that his work was mapped out for him at Kimberley. Gordon pressed him, and when he could not make him change his plans, observed, "There are very few men in the world to whom I would make such an offer. Very few men, I can tell you; but, of course, you *will* have your own way." On another occasion Gordon told Rhodes the story of the

offer of a roomful of gold which had been made
to him by the Chinese Government, after he had
subdued the Tai-Ping rebellion. "What did
you do?" said Rhodes. "Refused it, of course,"
said Gordon. "What would you have done?"
"I would have taken it," said Rhodes, "and
as many more roomfuls as they would give me.
It is no use for us to have big ideas if we have
not got the money to carry them out."

These two men of strong will used often to
disagree, and on one occasion Gordon observed
to the younger man, testily, "You are the sort
of man who never approves of anything unless
you have had the organising of it yourself."
Nevertheless, Gordon took strongly to the
young politician. His pressing invitation to
stay and work with him in Basutoland proves
this. Not long after Rhodes went back to
Kimberley, and Gordon shook off the Cape
dust from his feet and went back to Europe,
disgusted at the double dealing of the Cape
Government, which sent up troops through

Sauer to take the Basutos unawares, at the very time that they were conducting negotiations for peace through Gordon.

Rhodes, meanwhile, kept to his financial and political work, with the one great end in view. To this clearly-seen end, the winning of the vast hinterland, the possession of money and financial influence was merely the means, as was also the possession of political power from the very ·opening of his parliamentary career. In the Cape Assembly, in season and out of his season, he steadily devoted himself to his life-purpose. He soon found that he need hope for neither support nor encouragement among the Cape politicians in his schemes of expansion to the North. The Cape Colony was not then awake to the advantages of seizing the unmarked territory, and in England, our short-sighted party government, with its cheese-paring policy, was equally blind to the interests of our empire in South Africa.

As soon as Mr. Rhodes had settled himself in the saddle as member for Barkly West, he found openings for his forward policy. In 1882-3 he persuaded the Cape Government to send up a Delimitation Commission for the delimitation of Griqualand West, and went as one of the Commissioners himself. The difficulty with which the young Commissioner had to deal was the complaint of Mankoroane, the Batlapin chief, who ruled what is now Lower Bechuanaland, that part of his territory had been included by mistake in Griqualand West.

This Mr. Rhodes found to be perfectly true ; but as about seventy farms had been taken up in this territory it was impossible to return it to Mankoroane. Mr. Rhodes, with that swift and unerring perception of the right thing to do, which is a characteristic of his, as it was of Gordon's, obtained from Mankoroane a cession of the whole of his country, about half Bechuanaland, for the Cape Colony. Mankoroane, being hard pressed by the Boers, was eager to make this cession, as he would thus gain the protection of the Cape against his freebooting assailants. Rhodes returned to Cape Town with the cession of half Bechuanaland for the Cape; but the Cape, not then at all desirous of additional territory, refused the cession. What was to be done?

Mr. Rhodes, the guiding star of whose whole policy was already, in 1882, the idea of acquiring both Bechuanaland and the vast unoccupied regions to the North beyond Bechuanaland, was not to be denied. He had got the cession of this big territory; the Cape refused it; he would try the Imperial Government. Accordingly he urged the Governor to use his influence with Downing Street, and the Governor succeeded in inducing the Home Government to take the country on the terms that the Cape was to pay half the cost of administration. The Cape House did not care to pay half the expense when they had no share in the administration. Scanlan's ministry went out of office nominally for another reason, really because of the impossibility of carrying through the arrangement. The Imperial Government, however, established a protectorate over the territory in question in 1884, when Mackenzie was made the British Resident.

This Bechuanaland business is interesting as showing the continuity of Mr. Rhodes's policy of expansion. He began to push that policy to the front at the very opening of his political life. He obtained the cession of Lower Bechuanaland, as I have shown; offered it to the Cape, but found they would have nothing to do with it, pressed it through the Governor on the Imperial Government, who were at last reluctantly induced to declare a protectorate.

It was his experience on this and other occasions which made him certain that the Cape would not take over the Northern territories, on the possession of which the young politician's far-seeing mind was set; and he soon had further proof that the Imperial Govern-

ment could not be counted on for this work
of Imperial expansion, because, even if they
could have been persuaded of the ultimate
value of the country, they could not face the
expense of administration, much less the
enormously greater expense of development.
It was due to these lessons learned in the
efforts to carry out his scheme of expansion,
that Mr. Rhodes was reluctantly convinced
that his only chance of carrying out his policy
was the creation of a private enterprise—a
Chartered Company.

Immediately after the Convention of London
in 1884, President Kruger, who had only just
got the independence of his country, and had
not a sixpence in his treasury, with marvellous
audacity and foresight started upon his rival
scheme of expansion. Mr. Rhodes had already
made the first move northward in Lower Bechuanaland in 1882 ; but President Kruger was
no sooner sure of his independence than he
started out his lieutenants on every side to raid

and hold all the territory they could. One expedition was sent into Zululand, and successfully occupied the best of the country, and, there being no Rhodes in Natal to expel them, established the New Republic, and were in due course incorporated with the Transvaal. Another expedition, under Van Niekerk, pushed into Bechuanaland and founded the freebooting Republics of Stellaland and Goshen, with a town, in the latter called Rooi Grond. Mr. Mackenzie, the British Resident, vigorous and active though he was, was unable to cope with these resolute invaders, who knew what they had been sent to do, and did not hesitate to shoot. President Kruger next proclaimed a Protectorate over the territory in question, thus, as in Zululand, revealing in whose interests the Transvaal freebooters had seized the country.

Mr. Rhodes had already held office in the Scanlan Administration as Treasurer-General, when, in 1884, he succeeded Mackenzie as Deputy Commissioner for Bechuanaland, and had an excellent opportunity of using political power to forward his purpose of expansion to the North. In his last speech at Cape Town he has told us how, as British Commissioner, he met the Boer Commando that had seized Bechuanaland, and how he dealt with them. Resolute to keep Bechuanaland for England, he was quite willing to make large concessions in another direction. Farms the Boers might have and hold, but it must be under the British flag. "I know," said the oldest of the Boers to him, "that this is the key of South Africa." This was the truth, and it was because he was determined to keep for England that key to the interior that Mr. Rhodes was there. He kept the key for England, though it required all his efforts, backed by Cape Colony, led by the eloquence of Mr. J. W. Leonard, to make Sir Hercules Robinson act firmly. Had Mr. Rhodes allowed the High Commissioner to pursue his usual policy of peace at any price, the key to the North would have

passed into the possession of the Transvaal. It
is characteristic of Mr. Rhodes that he had
already offered a fair and conciliatory arrangement to the Dutchmen by which they were to
be confirmed in their farms; but this arrangement was refused by General Joubert, acting
on behalf of the Transvaal Government, which
had officially attempted to avail itself of
its daring filibustering enterprise by incor-
porating the territory. In the course of their
enterprise one English officer, Commander
Bethell, was murdered by President Kruger's
men, and numbers of natives under British
protection were slaughtered and their property
seized; yet not one penny of compensation
was ever paid by President Kruger or by the
delinquents themselves. Then it was that
Mr. Rhodes showed that while ready to deal
fairly and even generously with the Boers
individually, he was firm as iron on the
question of the flag. He at once insisted on a
display of force to retain the route to the North

and **expel** the fllibustering intruders.   Sir
Charles Warren's expedition was the result,
and Bechuanaland was preserved to the Empire.
Here Mr. Rhodes had his first encounter with
the Transvaal President's forward policy, and
came out of it a winner.

The fair-minded and conciliatory terms offered
by an Englishman had mightily surprised the
Boers, and perhaps laid the **foundation** in the
Dutch mind of that confidence in the "Englishman with the Afrikander heart" which **has**
enabled Mr. Rhodes to work successfully with
the Dutchmen of the Colony, and begin his
great work of welding together the two races
into one **united people.**

Thus early in his career **the** union **of** the
white **races,** the removal of race-feeling, was
a care to the young politician, combined **with**
an Imperialism, **as intense as** it was enlightened, which, acting **with** consideration and
justice, melted away by conciliation the opposition it would have been difficult to overcome

by force. And so it came to pass that Cecil Rhodes, in appearance, character, and sympathies the most English of Englishmen, was gradually accepted as the trusted representative of Dutch as well as English voting-power.

While Rhodes had been working to secure political power at the Cape, Gordon had not forgotten his independent-minded young friend. When he was starting for Khartoum on his difficult and desperate mission, he sent to invite Rhodes to come out and work with him in his contest with the power of the Mahdi in the Soudan. The keenness of the great General's reading of character was wonderfully justified when Rhodes last year went up on a similar mission into the Matopo Hills and single-handed achieved his object.

The day on which Gordon's offer arrived Cecil Rhodes had received the offer of the Treasurer-Generalship under the Scanlan Ministry; and, as this appointment lay directly upon the line of least resistance to the

end he had in view, he accepted it, unwilling,
though flattered no doubt by Gordon's
choice, to swerve for a moment from the
path he had marked out for himself.

If the future of the Soudan was upon Gordon's camel as he rode to Khartoum, the
future of British Empire in South Africa
hung upon this decision of Mr. Rhodes, without whom the expansion which has given us
the coveted empire to the North would never
have taken place ; for no one acquainted with
the facts would deny that the moving spirit
of the enterprise was the great statesman and
millionaire who had set this work of expansion
before him when a youth at Kimberley, many
years before, and had made himself, after years
of labour, the chief personage in South Africa,
both in finance and politics, with the unalterable purpose of carrying out his idea as swiftly
and effectively as possible.

I have now briefly given a sketch of the
main facts, and the unchanging purpose of Mr.

Rhodes's early life, and of the way in which financial and political power were obtained by him in order to subserve that purpose. By diamond-digging and finance he had already in 1888 made a large fortune himself, and had gained a most valuable influence with the millionaires with whom he had been associated in his various undertakings. And so when the Chartered Company was mooted in 1889, not only South African potentates like Mr. Beit, but world-famed financiers like Lord Rothschild were interested in the undertaking. By 1889, too, he had become the chief personage in politics at the Cape. He had early perceived that only by an alliance with the Dutch party could he hope to obtain the political support he required in order to carry out his idea of occupying the hinterland. He set himself, therefore, to win the Dutch; his plan being to occupy and develop the northern territory through the Cape Colony. In 1889, then, he had possessed himself of the requisite

instruments of financial power and political
power to enter on the great enterprise for
which he created the British South Africa
Company, and obtained a royal Charter.
In 1890, on the defeat of the Sprigg Ministry,
Mr. Rhodes, who was generally admitted to be
the ablest man of affairs at the Cape, became
Premier; thus combining in himself the management of the Chartered Company with the
political leadership of the Cape Colony. This
difficult position exactly suited his policy,
which was to use the powerful Dutch element
in the colony to aid his plans of expansion
towards the Zambesi, and, by carrying on
Imperial Expansion through the Colony, and to
its advantage, gradually to effect the reconciliation of the Dutch to the Imperial idea.

An alliance with Mr. Hofmeyr and the
powerful Afrikander Bond, was the first step
in Mr. Rhodes's policy as Prime Minister.
This secured the solid Dutch vote. It is probable that Mr. Hofmeyr intended to use Mr.

Rhodes to advance his own scheme of a Dutch supremacy in South Africa; but if this was his intention he was mistaken. Mr. Rhodes used his position so successfully that he gradually leavened the Afrikander Bond with his own liberal and enlightened Imperialism, and made acceptable to the Dutchmen of the Paarl the occupation of Rhodesia, though it finally cut off the Dutchmen of the Transvaal from the coveted hinterland to the North. As a working politician, he was soon as irresistible as he had been as an amalgamator of financial interests. Having arrived at the Premiership he intended to remain, and periodically depleted the Opposition by winning their leaders to his policy. Sir J. Upington became his Attorney - General, Sir Gordon Sprigg his Treasurer - General, two leaders of the Opposition being thus included in his own Government. Gradually the whole political ability of the Colony became united under his own dictatorship, and worked together for the benefit of the Colony, and through the Colony of the Empire, instead of dissipating their energies in party manœuvres and attempts to secure a party victory.

CHAPTER III.

THE OCCUPATION OF RHODESIA.

THE preservation of Bechuanaland, the direct trade route into the interior from the Cape, the key to the dreamed-of Empire of the North, had been, as I have shown, the work of Mr. Rhodes, during his Deputy-Commissionership in 1884, and his resolute grip upon the key of South Africa had been finally made effectual by the Warren Expedition. Germany had been encouraged by a growing ambition for colonial expansion to aim not only at acquiring the Transvaal but also the Empire to the North. This, as not even the Portuguese had any effective occupation, was open to the forcible attentions of the first comer in that scramble

for territory in Africa, which had already
begun among the powers of Europe. That
Mr. Rhodes should have been fully aware
that the old Boer was right who described to
him the strip of territory in Bechuanaland
seized by President Kruger's people as "the
key of South Africa," seems the merest matter ·
of course to-day. Yet we have only to look at
Froude's "Oceana," written after he had visited
the Cape in December, 1884, immediately after
Mr. Rhodes's intervention, to see how little
a man of great ability, and even some real
knowledge of South Africa, appreciated the
significance of the Boer filibusters' action.
Froude seems to have been utterly unconscious
of the value of Bechuanaland, and did not
even dream of the possibility of expansion to
the North, while Warren's expedition would
be, he thought, merely mischievous, if it were
not ridiculous. Of course Mr. Rhodes knew·
his South Africa better, and, with his eye on
the longed-for region to the North, would on

no account let the road to the North pass from under the British flag ; but the danger was a real one, for in Zululand, where Boer filibusters had at that time seized territory and called it the New Republic, Mr. Rhodes had no reason to interfere, the filibusters were not expelled ; and that territory, a large part of the best of Zululand, is now a portion of the Transvaal Republic. Thus in 1882, and again in 1884, Mr. Rhodes had used his political position to safeguard British interests, and by saving Bechuanaland had kept open the road to Matabeleland, and the immense territory to the North of the Zambesi.

President Kruger was not content with what he had done in Zululand and attempted in Bechuanaland. The resolute old Dutchman— whose daring forward policy Mr. Rhodes, always appreciative of ability and pluck, even in his bitterest enemy, could not help admiring— next sent up his emissaries to Matabeleland. Mr. Rhodes, hearing that the Transvaal was at

work to secure the northern territory, was
seriously alarmed; for he knew now with how
strong and bold an antagonist he had to deal.
But the young English Imperialist was equal
to the occasion. He hurried down to Grahams-
town, where Sir Hercules Robinson was at the
time, and urged him to get a treaty signed
with Lobengula.

Sir Hercules, good, easy man, would have
liked to be let alone. He said it was impossible
to make a treaty with Lobengula that took any
responsibility. Rhodes then urged him to get a
negative treaty signed, on the model of the treaty
made by the Natal Governor with the Queen
of Amatongaland. This negative treaty was so
called because it would merely bind Lobengula
to give the first offer to Great Britain, if at any
time he wished for a protectorate. It involved
no responsibility, but protected our interests,
resembling to this extent our right of pre-emption over Delagoa Bay. Mr. Rhodes's recom-
mendation was acted upon by the High Com-

missioner, and the result was what is known as
the Moffat Treaty, signed in 1888.

Mr. Rhodes was only just in time. The
Transvaal Emissary, Piet Grobler was thus
anticipated, and President Kruger's intentions
were openly made known when he produced unsuccessfully to Sir Hercules Robinson what
purported to be a treaty signed by the Matabele
King. Thus Mr. Rhodes by ceaseless watch-
fulness and activity succeeded in checkmating
President Kruger in Matabeleland, as he had
some years before checkmated him in Bechuanaland. The danger was great and real; for
Lord Derby had left open the whole of the
northern territories to be scrambled for and
seized by the first comers. Once more the consequences of the apathy of Downing Street
were prevented by the far-seeing and sleepless
patriotism of Mr. Rhodes.

What was he to do next in order to make
Moffat's treaty with Lobengula effective?
He had found by experience that the Cape

would not undertake a big work of expansion, and that the Imperial Government would not dare to face even a small fraction of the expenses of occupation. There was nothing for it, he saw, but private enterprise. Private enterprise, which had given us the Empire of India, was the one way open, he saw, to secure the Empire of Africa. With remarkable foresight he had mentally created the Chartered Company, long before it was mooted; and he at once set about obtaining the needful concession on which to base the Company.

On the 30th October, 1888, the Rudd Concession of the mineral rights of Lobengula's kingdom was obtained from that monarch by the tenacity of Mr. Rudd, and the keen and tactful diplomacy of Mr. Rochfort Maguire. The consideration of £1,200 a year, 1,000 rifles and a large supply of ammunition, seemed no doubt, magnificent to the wily old native despot, and he probably congratulated himself, with some appearance of reason, on having had the best of the deal. This was the celebrated Matabele Concession, which formed the solid basis of the British South Africa Company. Early in 1889 Mr. Rhodes came to London, and there made an agreement with the Directors of the Exploring Company on the grounds of their co-operating in support of the Rudd Concession through Mr. Maund, who had been up with the Warren Expedition, and had gained great influence with Lobengula. Mr. Rhodes, on his part, brought in the De Beers Company, which took a large interest (over £200,000) in the British South Africa Company.

In October, 1889, the Charter was formally granted, and the Company launched on its career of British expansion. It may here be remembered that the financial success of this great enterprise was by no means the certainty then that it seems now. The first subscribers were aware that the risk was considerable, had no notion that the public would perceive the potentialities of the scheme, and were on that account glad that in the subscription of the capital the De Beers Company and the Gold Fields of South Africa should do their part. This should be remembered in connection with the hostile criticism as to the allotment—criticism which is very easy to advance after the event, when the public have shown their high appreciation of the shares.

Already early in 1889, long before the Charter was granted or even secure, Mr. Rhodes, who was staying in London, was anticipating the uncertain future and endeavouring to secure a footing in Nyasaland by an arrangement with the African Lakes Company; for he had not the least intention of limiting himself, even temporarily, to Matabeleland and Mashonaland. The British Government, indeed, wished to restrict the Charter to the South of the Zambesi; but Mr. Rhodes, true to his dreams of Empire, with far-seeing ambition insisted on and obtained a free hand to the north of that river.

Interviews with Mr. Bruce and other representatives of the African Lakes Company resulted in an agreement by which the British South Africa Company's promoters (they had not yet obtained the Charter) subscribed £20,000 to the capital of the African Lakes Company, which had exhausted its resources, and also undertook to give Charter shares in exchange for Lakes Company shares, furthermore subsidizing the Lakes Company to the amount of £9,000 a year for expenses of administration. The British South Africa Company also obtained the right, on certain conditions, of taking over the subsidized Company—which it has since done—and Major Forbes, an able and active Resident, is now superintending the exploration and development of Northern Rhodesia up to Lake Tanganyika. Of course, Sir Harry Johnston's admirably governed realm was practically a portion of the same immense territory, and if it does not owe its existence, at least owes the finances for its development, to Mr. Rhodes.

Negotiations at Lisbon with the Portuguese were also projected, but circumstances caused an abandonment of the scheme. Enough, however, has been said to show the far-sighted and far-reaching ambition for the expansion of the Empire, by which Mr. Rhodes was inspired, even at this early period. His colleagues in general would have been much more modest in their aims, considering, from a business point of view, the question of expense and the certainty that such soaring ambition for expansion could not possibly prove remunerative—at all events, for a great many years.

The boundaries of the Chartered Company's dominion were purposely left undefined, in order that the utmost possible expansion over unmarked territory should be carried out; in

E

the slightly adapted words of Mr. Rhodes himself, who was the inspiration and the driving power of this vast patriotic scheme, "The great object should be to take as much territory as one possibly could." Of course, all this empire-building seemed wildly Utopian at the time, but the Empire-builder knew his own strength, and felt that no amount of territory he could get would be too big for him to assimilate. After events have proved that he was right; that he was as unrivalled as a consummate man of business in the development of territory, as he was unapproached in the range of his ambition for acquiring it. The ultimate aim of Mr. Rhodes then—as always since—was nothing less than to paint the map red for England over all unoccupied territory between Cape Town and Cairo.

The very first business of the Chartered Company was, in the opinion of its founder, effective occupation of territory; and, after some discussions with the famous hunter, Mr.

Selous, Mashonaland was decided upon as the first place for operations, and Dr. Jameson, an old friend of Mr. Rhodes, was selected to go up to Bulawayo and get the King's consent. This difficult business he accomplished with a courage, tact, and perseverance which won him golden opinions, a reputation which has been more than sustained by the extraordinary ability of his after-work as Administrator of the Company's territory.

Mr. Rhodes is emphatically a man of action; no time was lost, and under his direction a force of five hundred police was raised and a body of two hundred pioneers engaged to cut the road to Mashonaland. Colonel Penne-father was in command.

At Tuli a message met them from the Matabele King to forbid the making of a road; but the expedition pushed on through the thickly forested low country, where the work of road-making was most severe, and the risk of surprise by the Matabele most considerable.

Dr. Jameson went with the advance guard of forty men, that being regarded as the post of danger. Mr. Selous, knowing the country perfectly, acted as guide of the whole expedition, led the pioneers and cut the road. Fortunately the Matabele, being unprepared for such decisive action, made no attack, and on the 13th of August, by an easy pass discovered by Mr. Selous, the plateau of Mashonaland was reached, an open country where five hundred mounted men would have had no difficulty in coping with a Matabele army. Lobengula had done his best to stop the advance, but the pioneer force was out of the dangerous forest country before he knew, and the movement was besides very successfully masked by five hundred Bechuanaland Police, who lay on the south-west border of Matabeleland, and engrossed the attention of Bulawayo.

The occupation of Mashonaland thus satisfactorily accomplished, the neighbouring Manica was promptly added to the Chartered

Company's sphere of operations by a treaty
with the chief Umtasa, while no time was lost
in entering on negotiations and obtaining a
footing in Gazaland.

At the end of 1891 Mr. Colquhoun was
succeeded in the duties of Administrator by
Dr. Jameson, whose high qualities and sympathetic and unselfish nature soon won for him
not only the respect and regard, but the
whole-hearted devotion of the colonists of
Mashonaland. The early days of the development of a colony are generally marked by
hardship and trouble; and Rhodesia was no
exception. The settlers had at first to endure
great privations and discouragement. It was
a veritable inspiration that induced Mr. Rhodes
to appoint his friend, Dr. Jameson, to his
most difficult and delicate office, which he
filled with wonderful success; the readiness
with which he sacrificed, at the call of his
empire - building friend, the finest medical
practice in South Africa, being a fair index of

the devotion with which he threw himself into
this rough and arduous work. The ability
of Dr. Jameson's administration was as marked
as was its popularity with the settlers.

In 1892, after the rains, he got to work and
succeeded, by the most remarkable adminis-
trative ability, in reducing the Company's expenses from £250,000 to £30,000 a year. The
immediate prospecting of the mining wealth
was not more remarkable than the prompt
testing of the capacities of the country from
an agricultural and pastoral point of view.
On this bright horizon, however, one dark
cloud continued to gather and increase—the
outrages and insolence of native marauders
from Matabeleland. In July, 1893, they
pushed their murderous raids on the defenceless
and unwarlike Mashonas up to the outskirts
of the township of Victoria. Then, at last, Dr.
Jameson, who had contented himself unavail-
ingly with remonstrances to Lobengula, ordered
out a squad of police to restore order. The

Matabele fired on the police, and were promptly charged and routed. A peaceful arrangement with Lobengula had been attempted, but the dignity of the savage monarch was compromised; he was not to be appeased, and large forces of Matabele invaded Mashonaland. There were only forty police available, but the settlers rose to the occasion and formed themselves into a force with which Dr. Jameson determined to strike promptly before the rainy season came on. No time was lost in the preparations. The Chartered Company's funds were very low, in fact practically exhausted, but Mr. Rhodes, as usual, came to the rescue, and supplied the necessary capital from his private purse. He sold, I believe, among other assets, 50,000 Chartered shares at twenty-five shillings a share, in order to provide funds; sacrificing cheerfully, as he has always done, his private interests for the public welfare. The fact is, the financial pressure of the Company at this time was very heavy on

Mr. Rhodes's purse. He had raised the money for the Mafeking railway; he had just provided the money, out of his private means, for the Beira railway extension; he had found four-fifths of the capital for the Trans-Continental Telegraph; and now he had to find the money for Jameson's Matabeleland campaign.

The settlers, under supreme command of Dr. Jameson, advanced on Bulawayo in three columns, amounting altogether to some nine hundred Europeans. The first considerable engagement took place after crossing the Shangani River, when a large body of Matabele were repulsed, but the decisive battle was on the Imbebesi, where some seven thousand of Lobengula's best men were routed with heavy loss. The Matabele charged the laager in the old Zulu fashion, and machine guns and rifles quickly decided the result. Three days after, the Matabele capital, Bulawayo, was taken, while Lobengula, who had fled, was closely pursued by Major Forbes. This pursuit led to the most brilliant action in a war where the spirit of officers and men was always excellent. Major Wilson, with some eighteen men, afterwards reinforced by twenty more under Borrow, pushed on in front of Major Forbes, and, greatly daring for a great object, made his way into the midst of the King's army and right up to the royal waggon, eager to take Lobengula prisoner, and so end the war.

Being hard pressed by numbers he sent for help, which Forbes, himself attacked by the natives, and cut off by the rapid rising of the Shangani River, was unable to supply; and then Wilson and his men, refusing to abandon their wounded comrades, formed a barricade of their horses' bodies, and when their ammunition was exhausted, died fighting to the last. Forbes himself was obliged to retreat, but, after severe privations, was relieved by a column of one hundred men, who rode up with Mr. Rhodes from Bulawayo.

The fiery daring of Wilson's advance to seize the King, the dauntless resolution of his last stand, are simply the highest expression of the adventurous and chivalrous spirit that has distinguished the Rhodesians throughout; and of which there have been numerous instances in the fighting during the recent rebellion in Matabeleland. Certainly it is bare truth to say that no more brilliant campaign is to be found in the annals of our colonial fighting than the overthrow of the dreaded Matabele armies by the scanty columns of colonists who composed Jameson's Volunteers. The cost of the Campaign, too, amounting to not very much over £100,000, was not one-twentieth of what it would have been had Imperial troops been employed.

The Campaign thus ended, the Volunteers were almost immediately disbanded, and began to prospect for gold and select farms in accordance with the terms on which they had taken service. With such a body of settlers pro-

gress was extraordinarily rapid, and **Bulawayo,**
the capital of the new **country, quickly became**
the largest and most **important town** in Rhodesia.   Dr. Jameson, as administrator, **took up**
his residence there, and the richness of the
gold reefs and the large extent of highly
mineralised country within reach of the town,
soon **drew** together a considerable population.

CHAPTER IV.

THE WORK OF THE CHARTERED COMPANY.

AND now a word as to the good work which has been accomplished by Mr. Rhodes and the Chartered Company. This work may in the main be considered under two heads, expansion and development.

As regard expansion, the country to the North of the Zambesi has been secured and explored up to Lakes Tanganyika, Moero, and Nyasa, and treaties made with the chiefs to the North, as well as with Lewanika, the King of the Barotse to the West. Enormous mineral concessions have been obtained; the potential value is gigantic; but it will, of course, take much time before development in these distant regions can follow. South of the Zambesi, N'gamiland, a vast and little-known region, has also come within the Chartered Company's sphere, which, briefly, extends from the German sphere on the West to the Portuguese on the East. **It is more than** probable that but **for** the intervention **of** Germany and the German Government's **pressure at Downing** Street, Mr. Rhodes would have painted the **map red** and occupied the territory, even to the headwaters of the Nile.

As regards development, the record of the Chartered Company and Mr. Rhodes is still more remarkable; the Transcontinental Telegraph Company, a far-reaching idea of Mr. Rhodes himself, has **been carried** right across Rhodesia, and thence to Tete and Blantyre. From the last-named settlement the wire is already **being** carried to Lake Tanganyika, from which the next point aimed at will be Uganda, and **the** probable occupation of Khartoum by the Egyptian forces **will bring Mr.**

Rhodes's dream of connection between Cape Town and Cairo, so far as the telegraph goes, within measurable distance of accomplishment. Branch lines, like that from Salisbury to Umtali, and that from Selukwe to Gwelo, will soon multiply, when, with the arrival of the railway, settlers crowd in and towns spring up and grow.

The usefulness of this rapid telegraph development, for the conception of which, and also for the bulk of the money for the execution of which, Mr. Rhodes personally has to be thanked, has been proved at the time of the conquest of Matabeleland, and more recently during the rebellion in Rhodesia. Roads, of course, have been made in Rhodesia; but the all-important railway takes time. The line from Cape Town to Bulawayo is now being pushed forward at the rate of a mile and a half a day, and will easily be in the capital town of Rhodesia before the end of the year. The Beira line from the East Coast should reach Salisbury in Mashonaland, also before the end of this year. **Mr.** Rhodes has been using all his great influence **at the** Cape to push on the Mafeking-Bulawayo line, and thus to secure that cheapness of carriage which is essential to the successful working of the numerous well-developed mining **pro-**perties, which, **as** soon as they can get up machinery and **supplies by the** railway, bid **fair** to return **large** profits **to their** share-holders.

The Cape Colony, which, according to **Mr.** Rhodes's recent arrangement, **will** be deeply interested in working the railways of Rhodesia, will aid **in the** development of the Northern dominion **as** though **it** were **a** part of the **Colony, which will** have **a** free market in Rhodesia for its **farm** products, its wine, and brandy, shut out by prohibitive **tariffs from the** Transvaal. Thus the **frontier of** civilization will **be** pushed Northward more swiftly than before. Afrikanders **of** Dutch as well **as** of English descent have worked and fought side by side in Rhodesia, and it is a characteristic feature of the community under the sway of Mr. Rhodes, that race-feeling has disappeared, and the gallant services of Commandant Van Rensberg, Captain Van Niekerk, and the other Dutchmen of the Afrikander corps in the recent rebellion in Rhodesia, are as highly appreciated by their English comrades as if they too were English born. As Earl Grey truly observed, when complimenting the Afrikander Corps in his admirable speech at Bulawayo, at the disbandment of the Bulawayo field-force in July, 1896. "It is a pleasing fact that there is in this part of the world a complete sympathy between the English and the Dutch."

Mr. Rhodes has from the beginning of his political career worked for union of races, based on union of commercial interests, almost as vigorously as for expansion of territory; and it is interesting to note that it is exactly in the region in which his great dream of expansion has been realised most fully, that his policy of union has been most strikingly successful.

Fighting side by side against the Matabele savages, Englishman and Boer have learned to know and respect each other, and they will work in future side by side more heartily than ever, if that were possible, in the development of their common country. They utterly mistake Mr. Rhodes, who suppose that it has ever been his policy to set Englishmen against Dutchmen. The exact contrary is the truth. No one has done more to draw them together; for it must be remembered that even the Revolutionary movement was directed not against the Boers but against President Kruger's government, with its policy of selfish isolation, of deliberate separation of the white men in the Transvaal into two hostile camps in which what was the interest of the one was the loss of the other. This most important step towards the development of the Chartered Company's territories, which need the solid

F

work of the Conservative Dutchman, as well as the enterprise of the more progressive and adventurous Englishman, stands to the credit of the Chartered Company, thanks mainly to the influence of Mr. Rhodes.

Of course, in considering the accomplished work of the Chartered Company and Mr. Rhodes it is not enough to note, though it is worth noting, that all the material accompaniments of a high civilization are already to be found in the cities of Rhodesia. In the beginning of 1894 the natives' kraals were in ruins, and the Bulawayo of to-day had not yet sprung up, and yet in 1896 banks, hotels, clubs, newspapers, and a hospital, with a splendidly organised telegraph and postal service, had come into existence, while water would have been laid on by the Water-works Company, and electric lighting established, but for the delay caused by the Matabele rebellion. Mr. Rhodes has always regarded the telegraph-line, as it can be put up much more swiftly as well as more cheaply than a railway, as the advance-guard of civilization, and his faith, which he backed with his money, has been justified in the already active usefulness of his great Transcontinental line. Earl Grey and Dr. Jameson could testify to this from the point of view of the Administration.

The explorer or pioneer can hardly complain, seeing that even in the extreme North, on the shores of Lake Tanganyika, he can write home at the expense of twopence halfpenny postage, while he can receive a pound of tea or any other grocery by parcels post at the cost to his friends in London of one shilling. It is not too much to say that the speed and completeness with which the Chartered Company have developed their postal and telegraph system over a country in which England would be a mere district, is absolutely unapproached in the history of the modern world.

While town life is already thus highly organized, country life has not been neglected.

It has been from the first the aim of Mr.
Rhodes to encourage the settlement of the
country by South African farmers. On these
healthy uplands, in the South African air, the
white man can thrive and propagate his race,
and that race will attain to magnificent physical development. The Boers and other Afrikanders are living proofs of this. The Chartered
Company's quit rent of £3 for over three thousand acres of farmland is not exactly prohibitive. The experiment on a large scale of a
farm colony of white men by the Sabi River
has proved eminently successful, and the usual
agricultural products extend even to tobacco,
which has been successfully grown and is
already much smoked in Rhodesia. The two
colonies of Dutch farmers are equally well
satisfied with their experience of Rhodesia; for
as a pastoral country its veldt is unsurpassed in
South Africa, and this will doubtless be the
direction in which much of the farming of the
immediate future will go on, when once the

rinderpest has completely passed away, and fresh stock has been imported by way of Beira from Madagascar.

The treatment of the natives in Rhodesia—Mrs. Cronwright-Schreiner notwithstanding—is highly creditable to the Chartered Company. It would indeed be stigmatized in other parts of Africa as philanthropic to the verge of sentimentality. The use of the lash, for instance, is not permitted at all. Mr. Rhodes, who has always enforced total abstinence on the natives working in the De Beers mines, to the great advantage of their health, their morals, and their finances, has seen to it that the laws in Rhodesia against selling alcoholic liquor to natives are most severe, and the operation of the law has, under his sway, been so uncompromising that spirit-selling to the natives does not exist, a fact that honourably distinguishes the Chartered Administration almost alone among the many other European Administrations in Africa.

It may safely be said that the Chartered Company, if it has erred at all in its treatment of the natives, has erred by excess of leniency.

As regards the condition of the natives in Rhodesia, the stop put to the wholesale cruelties that resulted from witchcraft among the Matabele themselves would, if it stood alone, invest with beneficence the rule of the Chartered Company. But still more strongly is the change for the better for the native population brought out, when we remember the murderous raids of the Matabele on less warlike peoples. The total loss of native life in the recent rebellion was insignificant compared to the slaughter perpetrated on the Mashonas in any single year by Lobengula's destroying *impis*. Mr. Selous has described the cruelty and treachery which distinguished these raids upon the helpless and often unsuspecting Mashonas, and when it is remembered that Lobengula sent his warriors as far as Lake Ngami to massacre and despoil the Batauwani, and over the Zambesi River to raid the Mashukulumbwe or the Barotse, one gets an idea of the greatness of the deliverance which the Chartered Company has brought to the natives of South Africa. No doubt the Matabele themselves preferred the old marauding life, when they had a chance of getting women and cattle for nothing, besides washing their spears in the blood of defenceless villagers; but the repression of their indulgence in rapine and murder, though felt as a deprivation, can hardly be called seriously an injury to them; while the gradual substitution of labour for idleness will work altogether for their good.

Just as the Roman Empire conferred an immense benefit on mankind when it established the *pax Romana* over the warlike tribes of Europe and made development in civilisation possible; so the Chartered Company, gradually establishing the *pax Britannica* over its vast territories, is conferring an inestimable benefit on the inhabitants; for, as the tide of barbarism rolls back before the advance of civilisation, it is the many who benefit, and the few, the chiefs and kings, who suffer, deprived of their despotic power.

The territory over which this beneficent civilisation is being rapidly extended by the Chartered Company amounts to upwards of three-quarters of a million square miles. In the greater part of this territory the white man can thrive and increase, and the Chartered Company are rapidly opening up a region that will be invaluable as a suitable home to receive the fittest of the large overflow population of the United Kingdom.

If it were only for their work of acquisition and development regarded from this standpoint, the territory they have saved for England and are making fit for settlement by Englishmen, Mr. Rhodes and his Company would have deserved the deep and lasting gratitude of the British nation.

Furthermore, they have not only done a great work of development themselves, they have enabled others to carry it on elsewhere. Without the Chartered Company's subsidy of £10,000 a year, afterwards increased to £17,000, Sir Harry Johnston would never have been able to accomplish the admirable civilizing work he has carried through in the Central Africa Protectorate. The suppression of the slave-raids, the subjugation of the slave-dealing chiefs, that most admirable victory of humanity and civilization in Central Africa, has been won by the excellent little force of Sikhs and Zanzibaris officered by English guardsmen, for whose successful employment England has to praise the foresight and energy of Sir Harry Johnston, and to thank the purse, ever open for any good purpose, of Mr. Rhodes. It is true that this fertile region has now to supply its own expenses, but it has been tided over the bad times by the subsidy, the slave-raiders have been suppressed, the

country greatly advanced in material prosperity, and fairly well able to meet the demands for administration and defence. High
customs duties, however, unknown in the Chartered Company's territories, have now to be
imposed to raise the necessary revenue. The
fact is that nowhere is the genuine settler more
generously encouraged, nowhere is the burden
of the colonist lighter, and the advantages of a
high material civilization more open to all,
than in the southern and more developed portion of Rhodesia.

These advantages are, of course, made possible by the share in the profits of mining
enterprise. By an arrangement based on
Mr. Rhodes's idea that each prospector should
mark out as many claims for the Company as
for himself, the Company has fifty per cent.
interest in every mining property floated.
This interest has been very properly reserved by the Company to which the whole
mineral rights belong, which has spent mil-

lions in the acquisition of them and in the development of railways and other means of communication without which the enormous expense of mining would amount to absolute prohibition. The extent of the highly mineralised country south of the Zambesi, estimated approximately at four hundred miles long by from ten to thirty miles wide, should enable such a return of gold to be made, when the railways are up and living and transport of machinery are cheap, as will pay large dividends on a much more considerable capital than the Company has raised or seems likely to require in the immediate future. As time goes on and development proceeds in the plateau north of the Zambesi, the mineral wealth of that magnificent region will be opened up, and the profits available for division will increase indefinitely.

It is the knowledge of this, of course, which accounts for the fact that Charter shares, though not in sight of a dividend, are steadily bought by investors to lock up; and that 34,000 shareholders are not only willing to wait, but are ready to subscribe every fresh issue of shares, having confidence in the resources of the country and in the management of the great financier, the success of whose methods in the De Beers Mines and the Gold-fields of South Africa is visible to all. When the Mafeking line is up to Bulawayo, as it should be before the end of the year, and mines like the Bonsor, the Dunraven, or the Alice begin to crush regularly, the present shareholders will be able to reap in steadily increasing capital value, the results of their patience and their faith.

There can be little doubt, that if President Kruger perseveres in his present hostile attitude to the Uitlanders, and continues to carry out his promise of the redress of their grievances by passing such legislation as that designed to expel aliens or gag the press, the tide of European and Afrikander immigration will set strongly in the direction of Rhodesia, where, moreover, there are no monopolies like Lippert's concession of dynamite, no fancy rates on coal like those of the Boksberg railway, and, above all, no possibility of the confiscation of property by an unscrupulous Executive.

The more the work of the Chartered Company is looked into, the more favourably it will compare with that of any other similar company, and the day will come—it is not, I think, far distant—when the carping criticism to which the Company and its founder have been so long subjected, will seem as disgraceful to the intelligence or the honesty of the carpers, as it is disloyal to the Empire to which they belong.

The greatness of the debt of gratitude which England owes to Mr. Rhodes, as the originating mind and shaping hand, and to the Chartered Company, as the instrument he framed for the expansion of the Empire, will begin to be fully understood only when the immense value of Rhodesia begins to be realized, the value, not merely, I mean, as a gold-bearing country, but chiefly as a country naturally fitted for Europoan colonization, where English institutions and ideas, and English progress and prosperity are to be found firmly established. The plateau north of the Zambesi, as well as the bulk of Southern Rhodesia, form a region, several times the size of England, unsurpassed in the world for perfect climate, ample supply of water, grass, timber, and, in many parts, of coal, presenting in the main extraordinary advantages to the stock-breeder, and great attractions in numerous localities to the enterprising tillage farmer, and in the low-lying districts to the planter.

CHAPTER V.

It might have been supposed that Mr. Rhodes had enough and more than enough to occupy him in the colossal work of the development of the vast Empire to the North, which his foresight, enterprise, and daring initiative have secured as the heritage of future generations of Englishmen. In addition to this ever-growing work of development and administration, he had the business cares of the headship of such gigantic commercial undertakings as the De Beers Mines and the Consolidated Goldfields of South Africa.

He had, besides all this, the onerous duties of Cape Premier, in which capacity he had to deal with the highly important native question, itself one of the chief of the problems of South Africa. Though his Glen Grey Act may not be a final solution, yet it is certainly a very important approach to a final solution of the problem. Unlike other savages, the Kaffir or Bantu race tends to increase under the white man's supremacy, for the old check on population of savage wars and massacres has been removed. It is computed by Theal that not very far short of a million perished by the assegais and knobkerries of a single Zulu monarch in the early part of the century, while the extent of the slaughter perpetrated by the Matabele raiding expeditions is known to have been enormous, though impossible accurately to estimate. Two objects of the Glen Grey Act, of which some account is given in a later chapter, are to check overcrowding; and to encourage regular labour among the natives by discouraging that idleness to which male Kaffirs are prone. The working of this Act has, so far, been eminently successful; as might be expected from the sound common-sense of its author, and not less from his exceptional knowledge of the natives.

Mr. Rhodes thoroughly understands the natives, whom he has employed largely ever since he came to the Diamond Fields and super-intended his Zulu labourers early in the seven-ties. At a later date his management of them, on strict total abstinence principles, in the De Beers Mine, has been altogether bene-ficial to them, as well as satisfactory to the Company. The fact is, the natives thrive best under a beneficent despotism; they are simply big children, and the knowledge Mr. Rhodes obtained of native character, in his capacity of employer at Kimberley, and in his capacity of Secretary for Native Affairs, when he went among the Kaffirs continually and studied the problem on the spot, has, no doubt, had much to do with the extraordinary success of his negotiations with the Matabele rebels in Rho-desia, where he has peacefully brought the war

to an end, and is now known and esteemed by
the natives as their father and friend.

Engrossed in the solution of the native problem, in addition to his other work, Mr.
Rhodes has yet found time for practical labours
in the encouragement of the industries of the
Cape. He has studied on the spot, in France,
the question of the best method of dealing with
the phylloxera, which has already ravaged the
wonderfully productive vineyards of the Cape.
He has encouraged and fostered the growth of
the export fruit trade of the Colony, which is
likely, when fully developed, more especially
the export of grapes and pears, to be of considerable importance to the farmer, while he
has personally visited Constantinople, and by
means of an Imperial Firman obtained the best
Angora blood for the improvement of the
Angora goats, which are so important a part of
the livestock of the farmers of the Karroo.

It would be easy to multiply the evidences
of the untiring labours of Mr. Rhodes for

the benefit of South Africa, as well as for the expansion of the Empire. Enough, however, has been said to emphasise the statement, that through the whole of his political and public life Mr. Rhodes has been the hardest working man of business in Greater Britain. He lives in his work, and finds his recreation in undertaking more. Extraordinary capacity for work, a restless energy that must ever be up and doing, is as certainly a characteristic of Mr. Rhodes as an extraordinary tenacity of will; and it is the rare combination of these qualities, with the powerful imagination and intellect of a man of great ideas, that constitutes the solid personal basis of his greatness.

Mr. Rhodes ruminates an idea long and silently before he gives it a place in the practical programme of his life-work; but when once that idea has become a part of his policy, there is no man of affairs more swift and resolute in carrying his idea into the sphere of action.

In the midst of his multifarious activities the idea of South African Federation had for some years past occupied an important place in the then Cape Premier's scheme of work. Federation, it seemed to him, was the proper means to the end he had set before him of welding together the various states of South Africa into one people, on the model of the Dominion of Canada rather than of the United States of America.

In many ways the conditions in South Africa were, and are, eminently favourable to this scheme. Geographically, the States and Colonies of South Africa form a single vast territory without any great natural divisions or boundaries. The climate of the greater part of the country favours the development of the white man to a physical perfection superior to that found in any part of Europe. As regards population, there is a remarkable homogeneity; for the free Republics themselves were settled by the overflow of the Cape Colony. The

old Roman Dutch law is the common law
of all.

The irritating vacillation and ignorance of
Downing Street have, no doubt, caused racial
difficulty and racial feeling in the past; and
the internal misgovernment of the Transvaal
by President Kruger, together with his policy
of selfish isolation, have caused and are causing
yet more acutely the same difficulty and the
same feeling to-day.   But in the Cape Colony
and Natal, Englishmen and Dutchmen have for
years lived in amity side by side, and in
Rhodesia community of interests in the face of
common difficulties has drawn the bond yet
closer, and Dutchman and Englishman have
learned to trust one another as they fought side
by side against a common native enemy, and
have learned and are learning friendly co-
operation in joint efforts for the development
of their common country under the invisible
yet all - powerful sceptre of the influence
of one great leader, for whom they feel a

common trust and a common devotion. Thus there was and is everything to favour Mr. Rhodes's scheme of Federal union—excepting, of course, the Krugerite Government in the Transvaal.

Common commercial interests had already, in 1895, brought about a Customs Union for the Cape Colony, the Orange River Free State, and Rhodesia, and to some extent for Natal; and a Railway Union was in a fair way of accomplishment, thanks to Mr. Rhodes, though of course from this statement one must again except the Transvaal. Differences and distinctions of race are inoperative in the face of common interests and a common aim, and under a Federal Union local rivalries like that of Natal and the Cape for the trade of the Transvaal would no longer exist; the interest of each would be the interest of all. The native question again can never be dealt with perfectly except by common action, and if it were not to look too far ahead, Federal Courts would one

day immensely simplify a cheaper administration.

Of course in a Federal Union like that of the
United States of America or the Dominion of
Canada, citizens of one State would have the
same status in all, and the freedom of the
individual would be as well maintained as the
interests of the community. Recent events
have shown only too clearly that the centri-
petal force of Federalism is urgently needed to
meet and neutralize the centrifugal force of a
narrow Provincialism. Mr. Rhodes's Federalist
policy is thoroughly fair-minded and liberal.
He would deeply feel the disappearance of his
own flag, therefore he understands the feeling
for his flag of the Transvaaler or the Free
State citizen. Let him speak for himself.

"With full affection for the flag which I
have been born under, and the flag I represent,
I can understand the sentiment and feeling of
a Republican who has created his independence
and values that before all; but I can say

fairly that I believe in the future that I can assimilate the system, which I have been connected with, with the Cape Colony, and it is not an impossible idea that the neighbouring republics, retaining their independence, should share with us as to certain general principles. If I might put it to you I would say—the principle of tariffs, the principle of railway connection, the principle of appeal in law, the principle of coinage, and, in fact, all those principles which exist at the present moment in the United States, irrespective of the local assemblies which exist in each separate State in that country."

A Commercial Union and a Railway Union, then, is what Mr. Rhodes aimed at in 1894, when the speech from which I have quoted was delivered at Cape Town. He was satisfied that each State should keep its flag and maintain its local patriotism, its national sentiment; but he desired to consolidate the material interests of the whole of the States and territories of South Africa and wisely leave the rest to time. Of course it is obvious that this policy, if pursued, would in the end inevitably mean the British flag for all; but this would come about by a natural and peaceful process as the English population increased and the racial feeling gave way before closer intercourse. Unity of commercial interests would get rid of the expense and friction resulting from internal Customs boundaries; for, as in the United States of America, there would be free trade between the African States; the free interchange of the products of the various States. The vineyards of the Cape Colony, for instance, would supply untaxed the needs of the Rand, and the present monstrous import duties of the Transvaal Government on the simplest necessaries of life —for instance, flour, mealies, bacon, butter, eggs—would cease to extort a crushing taxation from the poorest class of English and Afrikander Uitlanders, the working-men of the community.

As a matter of course such united free trade would act as a powerful stimulus to the progress of commerce, and the Cape Colonists at any rate are, I fancy, by this time well aware how detrimental to their interests the contrary policy, the policy of President Kruger, has proved itself to be. At this point, it may be well to remember that Mr. Rhodes, though an enthusiast for Federation, is strongly opposed to anything approaching undue centralization. His attitude to Home Rule will be remembered; but an extract from the same speech, with which I have just now been dealing, puts his views plainly. "Even if, so far as the flag is concerned, we were one united people, it would be better so far as concerns the gold of Johannesburg, and the coffee, tea, and sugar of Natal, that there were a Local Assembly dealing with those matters." He is, in short, an Imperialist who believes in decentralization.

Of course he is fully alive to the importance of union, not only in the matter of tariffs, railways, coinage, and legal appeal, but also in the matter of the native question, to solve which in the Cape Colony, as we have seen, no one has done so much as himself, when he held the office of Secretary for Native Affairs, together with that of Premier of the Cape.

CHAPTER VI.

IN carrying out his broad and liberal scheme for the gradual development of a United South Africa under the hegemony and finally the flag of Great Britain, Mr. Rhodes had serious obstacles to contend with, obstacles which threatened, not only the immediate, but even the ultimate realization of his ideal.

First there was the danger which sprang from the ambition and activity of Germany. This ambition and activity did not begin yesterday, though the German Emperor's action in response to President Kruger's appeal, first drew general attention in England to the long-existing situation. As long ago as 1875, Ernst Von Weber, writing from South Africa, put before the then Kaiser and Prince Bismarck the German ideal for South Africa, which was revealed as the present Emperor's ideal by the searchlight of the events of January, 1896. This is what he wrote of the Transvaal :—

" What would not such a country, full of such inexhaustible natural treasures, become, if in course of time it was filled with German immigrants ? A constant mass of German immigrants would gradually bring about a decided numerical preponderance of Germans over the Dutch population, and of itself would by degrees affect the Germanization of the country in a peaceful manner. Besides all its own natural and subterraneous treasures, the Transvaal offers to the European power which possesses it an easy access to the immensely rich tracts of country which lie between the Limpopo, the Central African Lakes, and the Congo. [The territory saved for England by Mr. Rhodes and the Chartered Company.] It was this free unlimited room for annexation in the North, this open access to the heart of Africa, which principally impressed me with the idea, not more than four years ago, that Germany should try, by the acquisition of Delagoa Bay and the subsequent continual influx of German immigrants to the Transvaal, to secure the future dominion over this country, and so pave the way for a German African Empire of the future. There is at the same time the most assured prospect that the European Power, who would bring these territories under its rule, would found one of the largest and most valuable empires of the globe; and it is, therefore, on this account truly to be regretted that Germany should have quietly, and without protest, allowed the annexation of the Transvaal Republic to England, because the splendid country, taken possession of and cultivated by a German race, ought to be entirely won for Germany; and would, moreover, have been easily acquired, and thereby the beginning made and foundation laid of a mighty and ultimately rich Germany in the southern hemisphere. Germany ought at any price to get possession of some points on the East as well as the West Coast of Africa."

Though rather late in acting on Von Weber's idea, Germany has since then developed an ambition to become a great power in Africa, and as far as extent of territory goes she has been sufficiently successful. This success has been mainly due to the extraordinary apathy and ignorance which have been the distinguishing characteristics, until very recently, of the British Government in dealing with the future of our empire in South Africa.

Of course, if we look back as far as 1851 we find that the very notion of British expansion in Africa was scouted by the heads of the Colonial Office. Sir George Grey, who was appointed in 1854, saw the desirability of federating the various South African States under British hegemony; and the resolution of the Volksraad of the Free State proposing to reunite with the Cape Colony gave an opening which, if it had been used, would have peacefully consolidated our Empire in South Africa, for the Transvaal Republic would then, it is evident, have followed the lead of the Free State. The Colonial Office as usual threw away the opportunity, and cold-shouldered the great advocate of Federation.

Then came Lord Carnarvon's attempt at South African confederation on the lines of his successful work in Canada. He was fortunate enough to get the right man for the work in Sir Bartle Frere. Sir Bartle Frere set about his task with a full realization of its difficulty. But whatever chance there was of success, had Frere been loyally supported, the ignorance and vacillation of the successor of Lord Carnarvon, Sir Michael Hicks-Beach, made Sir Bartle's efforts ineffectual, and when Lord Kimberley came in with the new Liberal Ministry, the High Commissioner was left unsupported; the discontent of the disloyal among the Dutch was encouraged, and after the half-hearted attempt at coercion, which ended with Majuba Hill and the retrocession of the Transvaal,

Imperial influence and Imperial prospects in South Africa fell to zero.

An apathy and ignorance still greater, if that were possible, has marked the policy of Downing Street with regard to extension of territory. In vain did the Cape Ministry in 1875 urge the annexation of Walfisch Bay and the territory which is now German; and although Sir Bartle Frere induced Lord Carnarvon to consent to the annexation of Walfisch Bay alone, he could not carry through his larger proposals for annexation up to the boundary of Portuguese territory.

After the Transvaal war and the retrocession the Colonial Office policy was no better. " Her Majesty could give no encouragement to schemes for the retention of British jurisdiction over Great Namaqualand and Damaraland," wrote the Colonial Secretary. In 1884 this territory was, with England's consent and approval, annexed by Germany, and in 1892 a further portion of territory was added which carried the German flag to the Zambesi.

Thus, owing solely to the incompetency of our Colonial Secretaries, and in spite of the remonstrances of the Cape Ministry and our own Representative on the spot, we have handed over to Germany a territory four times the size of Great Britain. German South West Africa, the proper heritage of British Empire South of the Zambesi, remains a lasting memorial of what has been perhaps the greatest of all obstacles to the Colonial expansion of our Empire, the monumental ignorance and incapacity of Downing Street in dealing with its expansion, and indeed with all its needs, not excluding unification.

Prince Bismarck's words before the Reichstag Committee in 1884, are the best possible comment on this lamentable state of affairs: " No opposition is apprehended from the British Government, and the machinations of Colonial authorities must be prevented."

The same apathy and ignorance lost us Delagoa Bay in 1872; Lord Kimberley, in spite of the High Commissioner's warnings of the supreme importance of that harbour, insisted on going to arbitration, and though £12,000 or so might then have bought it from Portugal and avoided the arbitration, there was no Cecil Rhodes to find the money, as he has repeatedly done for the work of Imperial expansion (Rhodes was then a young man diamond-digging at Kimberley), and the British Government preferred to keep their £12,000 and lose Delagoa Bay.

Mr. Rhodes has, I believe, in later days unsuccessfully approached the Portuguese Government with a view to acquiring Delagoa Bay. Were Delagoa Bay British territory to-morrow the future of the Transvaal would be secure, the anti-British, anti-Rhodes policy of President Kruger would collapse, and peace and contentment be restored to South Africa.

The lesson of all this is, that the Colonial

statesmen who are in the country and know its needs are the proper guardians of its interests, and that Downing Street should be guided in its South African policy by the deliberate opinion of South Africa, not by the temporary exigencies of party Government in London.

This lesson it must, in justice, be admitted, the Colonial Office has at last taken to heart, and the consequence is that blunders of the magnitude of those I have adduced do not occur, and the forward policy of expansion goes on without serious interruption.

The possession of South West Africa merely whetted the German appetite for expansion, and accordingly, in 1887, Count Pfeil was dis-patched on a mission to Lobengula, from whom he was to obtain a concession like that which Mr. Rhodes obtained in 1888. Illness stopped Count Pfeil in the Northern Transvaal before he reached Matabeleland, but it is worth observing that it was through the Transvaal, not by the usual Bechuanaland trade route, that the German emissary approached Bulawayo.

Mr. Rhodes becoming aware of Count Pfeil's mission, lost no time in sending up his representatives, and succeeded in obtaining the Rudd Concession and thus preparing the way for the effective British occupation of what is now Rhodesia. Thus the most valuable unoccupied territory in South Africa was saved for British colonization and development.

Since then Germany has pushed her influence unceasingly in the Transvaal, and, owing to President Kruger's encouragement and support, with remarkable success. Germans and Hollanders, in alliance with President Kruger and his ring of reactionary Boer politicians, control the government of the country. Not only are important concessions like the Dynamite concession in German hands, but German capital has a preponderating influence in undertakings that are politically important, especially in the Netherlands Railway. It is, of course, this deliberate encouragement of German interference by President Kruger, this deliberately assumed attitude by which Pretoria leans on Berlin, that has made Germany for the moment England's rival in South Africa.

It would, however, be an injustice to President Kruger to suppose that he wants to forward the establishment of a German Empire in South Africa. He is far too shrewd for that. He does not want the Germans as masters; he wants merely to use their assistance to enable him to establish an independent and united Dutch South Africa, the headship of which, in virtue of its wealth, would naturally belong to the Transvaal. Thus his dream of a Dutch hegemony in South Africa bears a certain resemblance to the dream of Mr. Rhodes. The Cape Colony would be the centre and head of Mr. Rhodes's United British South Africa, the Transvaal the centre and head of President Kruger's Batavian dream.

The essential difference in their dreams is this. In the United British South Africa of Mr. Rhodes there would be room and representation, under equal institutions, and with perfect freedom, for the Dutchman. Racial feeling would be got rid of by treating Boer and Englishman exactly alike. Whereas in the United Dutch South Africa of President Kruger there would be no equality, and indeed no representation for the Englishman. Only Hollanders and Germans would be admitted, the Englishman and the Afrikander loyal to the British crown would be regarded as aliens, and treated, as the new immigration law reminds us, as if they were helots or Kaffirs.

Politics, for some time past and to come, in South Africa may be described as a duel between the rival dreams of unification, and their representatives, Mr. Rhodes and President

Kruger. The possibility of the success of President Kruger's dream would not be worth seriously considering, were it not for the immense weight and influence which its vast mineral wealth and rapidly-increasing population gives to the Transvaal. By the force of gravitation the poorer States of South Africa, the Cape Colony, the Orange River Free State and Natal, tend to be drawn into closer relations with the wealthiest state, which possesses the unrivalled gold mines of the Rand.

A Federation, of which the Transvaal was the head, would, if President Kruger were at the helm, be bitterly anti-English. There is not much danger, indeed, that Federation should take exactly this form; for in the Transvaal itself the Uitlanders already largely out-number the Boers, and the natural trend of numbers and wealth is towards the gradual absorption of the minority. But the Uitlanders are incensed and alienated by the weak and vacillating attitude of Downing Street. The unfortunate mistakes made during the intervention of Great Britain, through her High Commissioner, in the recent troubles, have with reason exasperated Englishman and Afrikander alike. And the danger is that a strong Anti-British Republic may grow up out of the combined Uitlander and Boer elements in the Transvaal, and form a permanent obstacle to that unification of South Africa, which is necessary, if there is ever to be a united South African nation, and without which there is no security that South Africa will keep its place as a part of the British Empire.

CHAPTER VII.

THE REFORM AGITATION IN THE TRANSVAAL.

THE present situation in South Africa is merely a further development of that long struggle for the hegemony which Mr. Rhodes, as representative of England, of English freedom and English institutions, has been waging for years with President Kruger, as representative of principles of government that are positively mediæval, and of an ideal which chiefly expresses itself in coercion and corruption, and in that unjust race-legislation which is calculated to foster and foment racial hatred. In the earlier encounters of this duel Mr. Rhodes had scored heavily. As long ago as 1884 he stopped President Kruger's attempts in Bechuanaland to close with his fiilibuster republics the trade route to the North. By his success in securing the Rudd Concession from Lobengula in 1888, he saved the hinterland, on which President Kruger undoubtedly had intentions, evidenced by the so-called treaty of 1887, which he unsuccessfully put forward.

Mr. Rhodes was not a whit too soon in sending up his young men to Mashonaland; for it was with not a little difficulty that the Boer expedition, under Colonel Ferreira, to seize part of what is now Rhodesia, was stopped by Dr. Jameson with his men and Maxims on the Limpopo. Indeed it is more than probable that hostilities would have occurred but for the powerful influence of Mr. Rhodes, on the Dutchmen at the Paarl; for the Transvaalers were furious at being out-generalled, and were strongly inclined to make a bold last bid for the possession of the Empire to the North.

The determined old Dutchman, whose

tenacity rivals that of Mr. Rhodes himself, was not done with yet. Headed off from the North he turned round and acquired, through his emissaries, a preponderating influence in Swaziland; and he had almost secured the possession of Amatongaland, which would have supplied the much-desired seaboard, when he was stopped, at the instance of Mr. Rhodes, by the then High Commissioner, Lord Loch.

Defeated thus to the North, the West, and the South, and defeated, as he was well aware, by the watchful activity of the great representative Englishman against whom the struggle had to be carried on, President Kruger cannot be blamed for the bitterness of his hostility, the measure of which is the keenness of his disappointment. Every South African is well aware that were Rhodes removed Kruger would sweep the board, and the progressive Cape Dutchmen to-day are eager to get Rhodes back, because, as they plainly put it, "We must have Rhodes to deal with Kruger."

President Kruger then had been hard at work attacking Mr. Rhodes in every way in his power long before the possibility of helping the Uitlanders to their rights as citizens had entered Mr. Rhodes's head. If one looks over the subsidized press of the Transvaal for the last five years, one finds ample evidence of this.   Indeed, ever since he obtained the Charter, Cecil Rhodes has been distinguished by President Kruger's sleepless hostility.

Long before Mr. Rhodes had touched President Kruger, the astute old Dopper diplomatist was assailing him through the organs he subsidizes, especially the *Diggers' News* at Johannesburg and the *Press* at Pretoria. Almost every week attacks were made in these papers upon Mr. Rhodes and his policy in Cape Colony, and upon the progress and working of the Chartered Company.

Nor did President Kruger stop here.

Within the Transvaal, at any rate, he could pursue his own policy unthwarted. If he could not buy Delagoa Bay, because of Great Britain's right of pre-emption, he could at least get hold of the railroad. Here he had a free hand, and here, if there were a secret understanding with Berlin, one would expect to find some signs of it. And here, in the capital and management of the Netherlands Railway, we find a clue to the anti-British intrigue with Germany. The capital was obtained chiefly from Germany and Holland, and not only was this the case, but a voting power, altogether disproportionate even to the large holdings of the Germans, was given to them, and Berlin with Amsterdam controls the Delagoa Bay railroad to-day.

The same hostility to England and England's suzerainty, marks the action of President Krüger in the internal government and legislation of the Transvaal. As long ago as 1891, Lord Randolph Churchill, in his letters to the

Daily Graphic, had observed the misgovernment in the Transvaal, and commented on the narrow selfishness and gross injustice of President Kruger's Government, and the wrongs of the oppressed English community, though he failed to perceive the far-reaching aims of President Kruger's policy. That the English of Johannesburg would, in a few years time, impatiently jerk from their shoulders the corrupt and unjust government of President Kruger, he regarded as a certainty, though the oppression exercised by the Boers was at that time far less intolerable than, by means of deliberately retrogressive legislation, it has since become.

All this is worth remembering, having regard to the misapprehension which has been widely spread and sedulously fostered by the Krugerite and Little Englander press, that the capitalists manufactured the Reform agitation at Johannesburg for their own selfish ends.

Since Lord Randolph criticized it the tyranny of President Kruger's Government over the

Uitlanders has gone from bad to worse. Indeed, from the first every change has been in one direction. At the time of the Transvaal retrocession in 1881 full citizenship could be acquired by the Uitlander after two years' residence. The first change was made in 1882, an advance of the residence required to five years. In 1890 the worthless concession was made of a Second Chamber, without powers with regard to taxation, or, indeed, any other important matter, while a change from five to ten years, and those not only of residence, but also of enrolment on the Field-Cornets' Lists, became the new condition for acquiring a vote, a change which excluded the oldest residents among the Uitlanders, as enrolment had never been before required or obtained.

In 1893 fresh legislation created a further change for the worse, by which, firstly, an alien may become naturalized after having been registered in the Field Cornet's books two years, and after the payment of a £25 fee. He then acquires the right to vote for the Second Chamber. After he has been in this position for two years, and provided he is thirty years of age, he is eligible for the seat in the Second Chamber. When he has been eligible for a seat in the Second Chamber for a period of ten years, he may acquire the full franchise *by a vote of the First Chamber*, and according to regulations to be fixed by law. These regulations have never been fixed, so that this tortuous and difficult path to the franchise ends, as was intended, in a *cul-de-sac*. This was hardly necessary, as the required vote of the First Chamber will always bar the way. To make matters worse the children follow the status of the father.

President Kruger, whose will has been and is law in the Volksraad, ever since his autocratic rule began, is responsible for this policy of exclusion, which shuts out the present generation of Uitlanders, and with them their successors, from rights of citizenship, and forms the present generation of Boers and their successors into a dominant caste, with absolute power over the far more numerous, intelligent, and civilized Uitlander population.

The absolute power thus placed in the hands of the Boers has been practically delegated by them to their strong old dictator at Pretoria, and is used by him without scruple or measure to extract a large revenue almost exclusively from the pockets of the Englishmen and other Uitlanders, who form the whole industrial class as well as the majority of the population.

Briefly, the Uitlanders pay about nineteen-twentieths of the taxation without any represen-tation whatever. The Boer, for his share, takes the voting, legislation, government, and spend-ing of revenue, and leaves to the Uitlander for his share the payment of the taxes. Mr. Charles Leonard has summarized the case for the Uit-landers with admirable lucidity and complete-ness. His summary of the facts up to the time when constitutional agitation was found

to be futile, and the Reformers were exasperated into employing the only cogent argument
with the Boers, a threat of immediate revolution, has done much to enlighten English
public opinion and remove misapprehensions.

Fortunately for the cause of freedom in the
Transvaal, Mr. Leonard, probably the ablest
man among the Reformers, succeeded in making
his way to England after the Jameson raid, and
has since then done yeoman's service for the
cause of freedom. A Cape Afrikander by
birth, a Uitlander by long residence at Johannesburg, he began his Reform Agitation in
1892, when he formed "The Transvaal National Union," of which he was chairman.
Thousands of the working classes at Johannesburg, with the bulk of the professional classes,
such as the doctors and lawyers, joined the
National Union, which aimed at obtaining by
constitutional means equal rights for all citizens, and the redress of all grievances and
abuses, while it expressly pledged itself to the

maintenance of the independence of the Republic. It aimed, in short, to make the Government republican in fact as well as in name, by the downfall of the present corrupt and tyrannical *régime*, which is a glaring anomaly, whether it be called an autocracy or an oligarchy.

In 1894 the Uitlanders petitioned the Volksraad, and the petition signed by 13,000 men was contemptuously received with laughter and jeers. In 1895 a fresh petition, signed by 38,000 men, a number far in excess of the numbers of the whole Boer male population, amounting at most to about 25,000, was rejected with contempt by President Kruger's obedient majority, though it was supported by a few Liberal members of the Raad.

This attitude of the Raad towards the Uitlanders is the work of President Kruger. He has been, generally speaking, ready enough to give the Uitlanders fair words and fine promises, but his unalterable hostility, which has found, and still finds, its true expression in legislation deliberately intended to render the lot of Englishmen in the Transvaal intolerable, found an authentic voice in his reply to the leaders of the National Union, " Go back and tell your people I will never give them anything. I will never change my policy, and now let the storm burst."

This attitude of uncompromising hostility had also found expression in open challenges to the despised Englishmen to appeal to the arbitrament of physical force, as when Mr. Otto, in the Volksraad in 1895, called them rebels, and told them they would have to fight for the franchise, and that he and the rest of the burghers were ready and eager for the encounter. Need it be said that such a challenge to high-spirited Englishmen was a direct incitement to take up arms, and one only wonders that they did not do so forthwith.

Crushed by excessive taxation, which fell with special severity on the working man, who had to pay, for instance, one shilling a pound on bacon and butter, sixpence a dozen on eggs, and seven shillings and sixpence on every hundred pounds of flour, while forced to contribute to the education of the Boers' children, and without any State aid to maintain schools for his own, it is not surprising that the masses in Johannesburg were ripe for rebellion, and the insults and challenges of the Boers, who vaunted themselves the proven masters of the race they considered finally vanquished at Majuba Hill, stimulated a deep resentment that only needed a leader to break out into open insurrection.

Up to this time, however (1895), though the professional classes had joined the movement, the forces of capital, always by nature conservative, had held aloof. The great mining capitalists, though the industry was greatly overtaxed by the excessive price of dynamite, under the Lippert Concession, and by the exorbitant rate on coal of threepence per ton per mile on the Netherlands Company's Boksburg coal railway, were unwilling to run the risks of supporting the agitation. Millionaires have too much to lose to favour the uncertainties of serious disturbance, and, generally speaking, the Rand millionaires much preferred the peaceful method of getting what they could by the use of "palm oil," which was fairly effective with, and highly appreciated by, their oppressors.

At last, however, in the autumn of 1895, the Uitlander Reformers, exasperated beyond measure by the contemptuous treatment meted out to them by President Kruger and his myrmidons, and recognising the hopelessness of seeking redress of grievances by means of constitutional agitation, determined, if possible, to unite to obtain their rights as citizens with one of the large mine-owners of the Rand, who was, they knew, a firm supporter of English freedom and English institutions, and who was also, they were aware, entirely above the greed of money, and might, therefore, be willing to spend his wealth as well as to risk his private interests for the sake of aiding his countrymen.

This mine-owner was, of course, Mr. Rhodes. The knowledge of Mr. Rhodes's record, the fact that he was the founder of Rhodesia, his well-known devotion to the Empire and the Imperial idea, his sympathy with English freedom and English ideals of government, made them hope that he might be willing to take the risk of aiding them, while the glamour of the great South African's reputation made them believe that his aid, if granted, would be certain to effect their deliverance from the grinding tyranny of President Kruger and his Hollander oligarchy.

The risk Mr. Rhodes had to take in helping them was, of course, great. He had to a great extent reconciled Dutchmen and Englishmen in the Cape Colony, and he was Premier and practically dictator there by the power of the Dutch vote. To help

Englishmen to obtain their rights from Dutchmen would be undoubtedly to imperil to some
extent his hold on his political supporters,
especially on the all-powerful wire-puller of
the Afrikander Bond, the representative of the
idea of Dutch Supremacy, Mr. Hofmeyr. Mr.
Rhodes characteristically put aside all personal
considerations, decided to take the risk, and
threw the power of his great personality and
commanding influence, and the free use of his
purse, ever open for any high and generous
purpose, into the struggle of the English
population of Johannesburg for their rights
against the intolerable tyranny of Pretoria.

In agreeing to help the Uitlanders Mr.
Rhodes was guided by the testimony of
Dr. Jameson as to the state of feeling among the
working men of Johannesburg. Dr. Jameson
had studied the conditions at Johannesburg,
where he had avoided the capitalists, and spent
his whole time in going about among the miners
and other workmen in order to ascertain their

feeling. He made himself certain that a revolt must take place before long, and the question was who was to guide the people? Jameson set about getting in the leading men and capitalists as leaders, only after he had felt the pulse of the people and ascertained their real feelings. Then, and not till then, he went with his report to Mr. Rhodes. Mr. Rhodes gave his support solely on Jameson's testimony; that the people, as distinguished from the capitalists, were eager and ripe to rise.

The object of the Reform Movement, which now set to work with renewed force, was simply to secure representative Government of the people, by the people, for the whole white population of the Transvaal, if possible by a mere display of a readiness to appeal to force, if necessary by making that appeal. Neither Mr. Rhodes nor the Uit-landers had any intention of forcibly interfering with the independence of the Transvaal Republic. There is ample circumstantial evidence of this, and, furthermore, the Reform Committee can produce irrefutable documentary evidence of the terms made with Mr. Rhodes, which consisted in an agreement to refer the question of maintaining the Transvaal flag and independence to a plebiscite, which would either vote for union and the British flag, as Mr. Rhodes hoped, or for independence, which, when Federation was accomplished, would mean a separate local government, but in the Federal Assembly of South Africa the British flag and admitted British supremacy.

The notion, put forward repeatedly by the organs that support President Kruger in London, that the Chartered Company purposed to annex the gold-fields of the Rand for its own benefit, is as obviously ridiculous as the statement that Messrs. Rhodes and Beit "made the movement and were thrusting it on their unwilling creatures at Johannesburg" is demonstrably untrue. The movement had been in existence for years, as I have briefly shown, and it was not until 1895 that Messrs. Rhodes and Beit were induced to aid it. The Chartered Company, though it was afterwards intended to employ its forces in the probable contingency of a rising, had, as a company, nothing whatever to do with, and nothing to gain by, the Reform Movement at Johannesburg. These misconceptions are probably scotched, if not killed, before now ; but there is one misconception that may still exist, which demands somewhat fuller treatment than I have yet given it.

It has been shown that the inception of the Reform movement and its working until 1895 were independent of capitalist aid ; and it may be added that in the Reform Union Committee of seventy only four were capitalists, and the rest professional men, who had nothing to gain and everything to risk by their action. In the face of such proven facts it might be hoped Sir William Harcourt would be by this time ashamed of misrepresenting the effort of an English community for the rights of free men by describing it as a mere stock-jobbing speculation. The misrepresentation now to be dealt with is very generally accepted, namely, the statement that the capitalists of the Rand as a body were behind the movement for their own greedy and selfish purposes. The fact that the house of the Ecksteins, representing Mr. Beit's firm, with Mr. George Farrar, and Mr. Rhodes, supported the movement gives colour to this statement; but a little knowledge is often misleading; and a glance at the ranks of the chief men of capital will show that only a minority of them had sufficient public spirit and sufficient daring to back Mr. Rhodes in his support of the popular agitation for the rights of citizenship. The bulk of the capitalists either held aloof from, or were actively opposed to, the campaign of the Reform Union. Mr. Beit's firm, by general consent the firm of highest character on the

Rand, was indeed on the side of reform. But Mr. Barnato's powerful house, with its enormous holdings of real estate as well as mines, had nothing to do with the movement, and Mr. "Solly" Joel's adherence at the last moment was strongly disapproved of by the founder of the enterprising Barnato Bank.

Opposed directly to Mr. Beit's house, as an uncompromising backer of President Kruger, was that many-millioned mine-owner, Mr. J. B. Robinson. Mr. J. B. Robinson had, of course, not the slightest interest in the cause of free institutions and equal representation for an English population; and he had used and uses his considerable power in the press his wealth controls, to aid the Government of President Kruger and to strike at his personal enemies, of whom none is regarded with keener hostility than Mr. Rhodes. It is believed by many that Mr. Robinson's ambition is confined to mere money-getting, which sometimes ensures a very limited measure of

social success ; but, in addition, it is not improbable that a desire to succeed President Kruger
as President of the Transvaal may have something to do with his attitude.   At all events he
is a stout supporter of the present *régime* at
Pretoria, and his immense wealth, hard business
ability, and great power in the press, make his
support highly valuable.

With Mr. J. B. Robinson, as supporters of
President Kruger, must, of course, be ranked
the representatives of German capital, such as
Messrs. Albu and Berlein; and on the same
side, or at any rate holding aloof from the
Reform Union, were hosts of minor millionaires.

Thus it may be seen that the majority of the
capitalists of the Rand were not combined to
support the Reform Union, as has been erron-
eously asserted, but rather were either hostile
or indifferent to it.   The Reform movement
was, in short, spontaneous and popular, and
the capitalists, Mr. Rhodes and Messrs. Beit,
Phillips, and Farrar, joined it only when con-

stitutional agitation had been tried and proved to be ineffectual, and money was needed for a demonstration of the forces latent in the movement.

But it is not enough to show that the Reform movement was not a mere selfish game of grab, organised by the capitalists of the Rand. The misrepresentation has gone further. A suspicion has been sedulously disseminated by the Krugerite press, and very generally entertained, not only that the great financiers intended to seize the Rand for the benefit of the Chartered Company—a notion too ridiculous to need refutation—but that they actually sold "bears" of large blocks of mining shares, knowing that the rising would cause a collapse in prices, as its failure undoubtedly did. But a moment's reflection should dispose of this theory as untenable. It is contrary to reason to suppose that those who joined and financed the movement to make it a success, and who aimed at and expected success, should have speculated to secure large profits if it proved a failure. As for Mr. Beit's firm (Wernher Beit & Co.), their record alone should dispose of such suspicions. In the great "boom" of 1895, they might have made colossal profits by floating untried and unproved properties. It was a matter of common knowledge at Johannesburg that they did nothing of the kind. The credit of their high reputation, as the first firm on the Rand, the most careful to test a property before taking it up, the most vigilant to provide against all probabilities of failure, was maintained with scrupulous attention, while other capitalists were hurrying out untested properties, for instance, in the Heidelberg district alone, properties to the extent of many millions, in some of which shares that then stood at £5 are now worth as many shillings. Furthermore, it is no secret that Mr. Beit has offered to allow the inspection of his books by the Parliamentary Committee.

The explanation, probably, of this suspicion

is to be found in the fact that so large a number of persons in England and on the Continent were hit by the unexpected fall that followed the Jameson catastrophe, and were eager to accept any theory that seemed to account for their losses. Besides, the fallacy *post hoc ergo propter hoc* is as old as human nature. While of equally faulty reasoning, the conclusion jumped at from the use (obviously to avoid suspicion) of the common terms of the mining market in the cypher telegrams, that the movement was a mere financial conspiracy, is an amusing example.

Just as all this talk of a financial conspiracy is very wide of the truth, so the accusation of buying off the hostility, and buying up the support of the press, and "salting," as Mr. Arnold Foster terms it, the House of Parliament, is mere wild and reckless conjecture. The fact that the big financiers like Mr. J. B. Robinson are quite as numerous on President Kruger's side as against him, and the remembrance of the huge secret service fund at the disposal of the Transvaal Government, which unquestionably has subsidized the Krugerite press in the Transvaal, if not in London, will make reasonable men consider that the accusation might be made with greater probability against the opposite side, or at least will make them pause before they accept these confidently-made, but absolutely unsupported, accusations.

The truth is that a monstrous campaign of malicious misrepresentation has gone on for a long time past in the English press against Mr. Rhodes and the Chartered Company. Whenever there has been an opportunity of testing these accusations they have proved to be ridiculously, as well as maliciously, false. Mr. Rhodes, for instance, was held up to obloquy by more than one London newspaper as a sneaking coward, whose cowardice was so flagrant that it was known wherever he was known in South Africa.

The Matabele insurrection has since then

supplied an unexpected test; and the much-maligned Mr. Rhodes turns out to be a man of the greatest coolness and fearlessness under fire, as was proved at Shiloh and Thabas Imamba, while by his daring in riding, unarmed and unprotected, into the fastnesses of the Matabele rebels in the Matoppos, and risking capture or death in order to put an end to the war, he has established a record which the bravest soldier might be proud of. It may be added that his weeks of sojourn close to the rebels in an unguarded camp, which might have been rushed any night, prove his courage to be of an even higher and rarer temper.

One would hope that his calumniators were now heartily ashamed of themselves, but that experience unfortunately does not encourage this hope. The scandalous accusations levelled at the Chartered Company in regard to the first Matabele war are an instance of the experience I refer to. An official inquiry knocked the bottom out of these accusations; yet Mr. Labouchere has steadily continued to pour them out, regardless of the finding of the official Inquiry.   This sort of decent and fair-minded criticism first clamours for an official inquiry, and when that is given, and the whole arraignment is proved to be a farrago of malice and mendacity, goes on repeating it with brazen effrontery.   One cannot but anticipate that the same action will follow the Parliamentary Inquiry, and if Mr. Chamberlain thinks thus to clear himself from the unfounded aspersions of his critics, he will, it is to be suspected, find himself completely mistaken.

CHAPTER VIII.

THE RAID.

RETURNING to the connection of Mr. Rhodes with the work of the Reformers at Johannesburg, it must be noted here that in the Autumn of 1895 circumstances had brought President Kruger and the Premier of the Cape Colony into somewhat more acute antagonism than usual. In pursuance of a policy by which President Kruger intended to bring the Cape Colony to its knees before the Transvaal, the rates charged by the Transvaal Government on goods coming from Cape Colony to the Rand had been, by leaps and bounds, quadrupled, in spite of a verbal agreement made with Sir J. Sivewright, by which the Transvaal President, as consideration for a loan to build the railway, had agreed not to raise the rates. When the rates were quadrupled, they became prohibitive, as President Kruger intended, his purpose being to divert the traffic to his German-Dutch railroad from Delagoa Bay.

In order to defeat this purpose the goods were transferred on the Cape Colony frontier to waggons, which drew them across the Drifts to the Rand. President Kruger was not to be beaten so easily. He deliberately closed the Drifts. This raised the whole Cape Colony, for not only would the Cape producer suffer, but the Cape railroads would be ruined if this policy was adhered to. Mr. Chamberlain was appealed to by Sir Hercules Robinson, and after obtaining the consent of the Cape Colony, through its Premier, Mr. Rhodes, to bear half the cost, if war should ensue, the Secretary for the Colonies launched an ultimatum, which forced President Kruger to re-open the Drifts. President Kruger, be it observed, though obstinate, has always been manageable by an ultimatum. This was the means by which the incorporation of the filibustering republics in Bechuanaland with the Transvaal was stopped some thirteen years ago, and this instrument of peaceful coercion will not improbably have to be used again by Mr. Chamberlain in the near future.

The threat of war threw the Kruger Government into the arms of Germany, and Dr. Leyds was soon at Berlin on a secret mission, the purpose of which it is not hard to conjecture. The Uitlanders had been highly incensed and alarmed by the stopping of their supplies through the closing of the Drifts, and this despotic action of the Transvaal President strengthened the hands and hastened the preparations of the Reform Union.

Meanwhile Mr. Rhodes had sent his trusted and skilful lieutenant, Dr. Rutherfurd Harris, to obtain from Mr. Chamberlain permission to station the Chartered Police at Gaberones, to protect the extension of the Mafeking railway;

a purpose in which at first he was unsuccessful. At a later date, when a division of the Bechuanaland Protectorate was made such as to satisfy Khama and the other chiefs, though only a strip of territory on the Transvaal frontier was given to Mr. Rhodes and the Chartered Company, the Bechuanaland police were transferred to the Company without further difficulty.

Dr. Jameson massed the Bechuanaland police at Mafeking, and got together a small police force from Bulawayo at Pitsani Pothlugo, a suitable camp in Montsioa's country, in order that should the threatened insurrection break out at Johannesburg he might be ready to ride in and assist in establishing order and a stable government; somewhat as Lord Loch had purposed to do with the Bechuanaland police in 1894. The differences in the position were these. Mr. Rhodes, as Cape Premier, acted to some extent without the official knowledge of the High Commissioner, whose approval would have made all these precautions perfectly regular, and who was, certainly, perfectly aware of the impending revolution at Johannesburg, and perhaps not altogether ignorant of the preparations. He, of course, intended also to use Jameson's force to ensure the success of the insurrection in the Transvaal. Possibly Mr. Rhodes may have remembered that Shepstone annexed the Transvaal without the knowledge of Sir Bartle Frere, the High Commissioner, who did not receive the Proclamation till a fortnight after it was published; but who, though he personally disapproved of its terms, kept his views to himself and loyally supported Shepstone, considering it to be in the interests of the Empire to support at any cost an official on the spot who might be assumed to have acted for the best.

Dr. Jameson made his preparations as well as he could in the time and handicapped by the conditions; but succeeded in getting together an utterly inadequate force of men for the proposed intervention at Johannesburg. Meanwhile arms and ammunition were smuggled into Johannesburg; but in altogether insufficient quantities—yet, strange to say, without any misgiving among the Reformers.

The Reformers, in fact, seem to have undervalued the fighting power of the Boers almost as completely as did Dr. Jameson. At the same time, the leaders of the Revolutionary Movement had not been as idle or unreasonably self-confident as has been often asserted. It can do no harm now to reveal the chief enterprise by which they proposed at once to supply their own need of arms and ammunition, and, at the same time, to deprive the Boers of their most powerful weapon of offence. The arsenal at Pretoria, with the batteries of Krupp artillery, was guarded so inadequately that it was perfectly plain that it could be "rushed" by a few hundred resolute men from Johannesburg. To surprise the arsenal and carry off its contents was the chief offensive movement in the

Johannesburghers' revolutionary plan of campaign. This scheme, however, failed to come off for one reason or another.

This alone would have been bad enough; but the paralysing effects of suspicion had also begun to make themselves felt throughout the ranks of the Reformers. A revolution directed by a Committee is proverbially without a head, and if four was just three too many, what could be expected when they added to themselves forty? The belief, due to a complete misunderstanding on the part of one of the Reformers, that Mr. Rhodes insisted on the hoisting of the British flag, rapidly gained ground. The Uitlanders had come into the movement on the supposition that the independence of the Transvaal and the Republican flag would be maintained. At a meeting of the leaders it was decided unanimously to send Mr. Charles Leonard, the chairman of the Reform Union, to see Mr. Rhodes at Cape Town. Meanwhile, rumours flew through the ranks of the revolution as to the supposed change by which Mr. Rhodes intended to use the movement for reform as a tool to enable him to annex the Transvaal for the Imperial Government.

South Africans have bitter memories of the apathy and vacillation of Downing Street, and the discontented Uitlanders, though determined to overthrow President Kruger's oppressive government, had, many of them, not the slightest intention of divesting themselves of their independence and hauling down the State flag, which, hopeful as they were of getting representative government by force, if not by constitutional agitation, they saw no reason to put away. Besides, although many of the Reformers, being English by birth or descent, would personally have preferred the old flag, yet even these were bound by the terms on which they had induced some of the others, who were ardent Republicans, to join the movement, of which the accepted object was to make the Transvaal a free Republic, in fact as well as in name.

Mr. Leonard saw that a complete paralysis of distrust, due to this rumour of a change in the purposes of the revolution, was spreading through the revolutionary party and making united action, of which the very first essential is mutual trust, a manifest impossibility. Accordingly, he was perfectly willing to go down to Cape Town and see Mr. Rhodes, the more so because he was convinced that Mr. Rhodes was not the man to break faith, still less insist on terms which inevitably involved a breach in the revolutionary party, and were, moreover, certain to lead to serious complications. Mr. Leonard, then, went hastily down to Cape Town and found that Mr. Rhodes had been completely misrepresented.

Mr. Rhodes had never had any intention of insisting on the acceptance of the British flag; he considered it perfectly reasonable and right that the Transvaalers, if they liked, should

retain their independence. All that he wanted
was equal representation and equal rights for
the citizens—whether Dutch, English, or any
other nationality. The rest, he said, would
follow in due time. Let the question be submitted to the will of the people expressed in
a plébiscite, was his arrangement with Mr.
Leonard; either they will vote for immediate union—and that means the British flag
—or else they will keep their independence,
which will be simply local self-government
with a separate flag—but even in this case
the flag of Federal South Africa must be
British, for the majority of States in the
Federation—Cape Colony, Natal, Rhodesia—
will send delegates who will unquestionably
insist on the British flag. The immediate
result of the revolution would be, at worst, a
progressive government, elected by the majority
of the people, a liberal President, and a liberal
policy, which would bring the South African
Republic into the ranks of South African

progress, and enable it at any rate to join the Customs and Railway Union of the other States, and hasten, by the rapid growth of population that would follow, the building up of a United South Africa, under the hegemony of Great Britain.

When Mr. Leonard had explained to Mr. Rhodes the collapse of the plot to seize the arsenal at Pretoria, and the inadequate supply of arms and ammunition, Mr. Rhodes at once saw the reasonableness, and indeed the necessity of a postponement of the rising at Johannesburg.

Recognising the difficulty, Mr. Rhodes pointed out that the delay would do no harm. " You can try peaceful methods first; and I can keep Jameson on the frontier," he said, "six months or nine months, it matters not how long, till your plans and your armament are complete, and your action will have a reasonable prospect of success." Any delay seemed better to Mr. Rhodes than that deficient organization or equipment should wreck the broad scheme he had framed at Groote Schuur in the interests of Transvaal freedom, and South African Federation, under the British flag.

The rising, then, had been given up for the time being. The Transvaal Reformers, reassured by telegram, were to learn fully from Mr. Leonard, on his return to Johannesburg, the exact attitude of Mr. Rhodes towards the independence of the Republic, and the cheering certainty that if it took six months for them to complete their preparations and mature their plans, they would, at the close of that time, find Jameson's column still lying on the frontier, and ready to ride in to the aid of Johannesburg so soon as Jameson learned that an insurrection had taken place there, and a force of trained men was required to restore and maintain order. Mr. Rhodes, satisfied with the turn things had taken, had telegraphed to Jameson that the revolution was for the time being postponed, for Johannesburg

L

was against any immediate action; and Mr. Leonard was preparing to return to Johannesburg and report fully the result of his negotiations to his colleagues of the Committee. This was the situation on December 28th at Cape Town, and the knowledge of this situation had been, of course, immediately transmitted to the Uitlanders at Johannesburg.

The situation at Johannesburg was, of course, greatly ameliorated by the news of Mr. Rhodes's attitude, and by the abandonment of the projected appeal to arms just arranged between Mr. Leonard and Mr. Rhodes. The knowledge that Pretoria was on the alert, and the fact that they had not weapons for more than one man in ten, or cartridges for more than a few hours' fighting, made not only experienced officers like Colonel Rhodes, but also sensible civilians, realize the futility of a rising. As that was postponed all might now go well. Everyone naturally felt relieved at this decision.

The plans of the Uitlanders having thus been deranged by a series of mischances, they proposed to attempt to obtain the desired reforms by mere demonstration without any immediate resort to arms. They lost no time in telegraphing to Jameson and sent messengers to explain to him, both by letter and word of mouth, that he was on no account to move across the frontier. Telegrams, practically to the same prohibitory effect, were sent to him by Dr. Harris for Mr. Rhodes; but Jameson's replies already began to show impatience. He found that he could not keep his men together, and it was soon plain to him that, if he did not move at once, he would not be able to move at all. Moreover, he began to suspect that the Boers were not quite so simple as to suppose that his force was held on the frontier merely to protect the railway. As a matter of fact the breastworks at Krugersdorp show that the Boers anticipated the line of his advance nearly a fortnight before.

The date for the rising had been fixed, but Pitsani and Cape Town were, as has been seen, fully informed of the postponement at Johannesburg. To insist on immediate action, was in the opinion of the wisest heads at Johannesburg to ensure a fiasco. Mr. Charles Leonard had satisfied Mr. Rhodes that an abandonment of the plan of revolution, for the time being at any rate, was imperative. Mr. Rhodes had found the reasons amply sufficient, and agreed not only to a postponement but to the attempt to obtain by peaceful negotiations the reforms that were originally to have been wrested from President Kruger by a display of force. The High Commissioner himself had telegraphed to Mr. Chamberlain that the revolution had fizzled out like a damp squib. Mr. Rhodes satisfied to wait, and Mr. Leonard satisfied with the result of his mission to Groote Schuur, were suddenly electrified by Jameson's telegrams of December 28th and 29th, which arrived together. The telegram of December 28th ought to have

arrived before; its late arrival was the fatal circumstance which brought about the catastrophe
of Mr. Rhodes's true intentions not reaching Dr.
Jameson. It was to this effect: "Unless I hear
definitely to the contrary shall leave to-morrow
evening for the Transvaal." The telegram of
December 29th ran to the same effect: "Shall
leave for Transvaal to-night." These telegrams
informed Mr. Rhodes, on December 29th, that
Jameson had decided to cross the frontier.
These telegrams arrived on Sunday, and Mr.
Rhodes at once replied to them, unmistakably
forbidding any advance, and expressing his hope
of a peaceful solution. " Things in Johannesburg I yet hope to see amicably settled, and
a little patience and common-sense is only
necessary. On no account whatever must
you move. I most strongly object to such a
course." The fates again were adverse; and Mr.
Rhodes's telegram, which, had Jameson received it, might just possibly have stopped him,
though handed in at the office by Mr. Stevens

could not get through, as on Sunday morning the office at Mafeking was closed, and on Sunday evening Jameson had cut the wires. Jameson having thus given full notice, and guarded against prohibition, started on Sunday, so that when the wires were repaired on Monday, it was useless for **Mr.** Rhodes to telegraph, as the column was a day and a night's hard march on the way to Johannesburg.

Thus Jameson, to use Mr. Rhodes's metaphor, took the bit in his mouth and bolted. He might better have considered himself to be only an auxiliary, and the Reform leaders who represented Johannesburg to be the principals. He ascribed the difficulties they alleged to mere fear, **and** the course of his **thought** may be traced in the telegrams collected in the Cape Blue-Book. Lack of courage he considered to be the real hitch at Johannesburg, and he proposed to supply the necessary stimulus by riding in with this column, whether the leaders liked it or not. As he telegraphed to Dr. Rutherfurd

Harris on December 28th, "There will be no flotation if left to themselves. First delay races which did not exist; second policies already arranged. All mean fear."

Thus it was that Jameson, judging, naturally enough, that a Committee now watered down with forty additional members would be wanting in strength and decision, determined to supply the necessary leader by coming in himself. Had he succeeded in getting through, all, he still thinks, would have gone well. He would at once have opened negotiations with President Kruger, and arranged to take a plebiscite of the inhabitants of the Transvaal. This would have resulted in the election of a Liberal Boer or Englishman as President, and in the establishment of free institutions and all the desired reforms. The Transvaal would have got into line with the Cape. The unification of South Africa would have been accomplished.

This was the end which Jameson felt to be within his reach. His men could not much

longer be kept in hand; it was now or never;
and he could not make up his mind to accept
the latter alternative. He had had no reply to
his telegram of December 28th, and, therefore,
there could, he thought, be no serious hitch.
He had somehow come to regard the enterprise
as certain of success; and his ardent Imperialism could not brook the thought that
only a little wilfulness on his part was needed
to remove the last obstacle to the union of
South Africa.

In his entire absence of self-interest he was
perfectly willing to take all the risks and bear
all the blame. He forgot that there were risks
for others involved, and that the blame would
not fall on him alone. From the first misfortune
dogged the steps of the column. The obvious
precaution of cutting the wires to Pretoria had
been taken; but the troopers sent to do the
work got drunk at a store, and left their work
undone, and thus the news of the invasion
reached President Kruger immediately. The

long ride, day and night, without rest wore
out both horses and men. At Krugersdorp
the position was occupied at first by five
hundred Boers, but reinforcements were continually arriving, for the whole country-side
was alarmed. Here Jameson was met by a
cyclist messenger from Johannesburg with
letters, the contents of which cheered the tired
troopers, and led to a front attack on Krugersdorp. Willoughby, who was in command, is a
careful student of tactics, and condemned to
Jameson the front attack from a tactician's
point of view, but held himself bound to co-
operate, as he was asked, with the supporting
attack from Johannesburg on the Boer rear.
Krugersdorp had been the trysting-place from
which the Uitlanders were to guide the column
in. Of course the Reform leaders are not responsible for this fiasco; as they had been at
cross-purposes with Jameson for the preceding
week, he, eager to come in at once, they urging
postponement. The day was thus wasted in

attacking Krugersdorp, when it might easily
have been used in getting to their journey's
end, by making a *détour* and avoiding the Boer
position. When they did at last resolve to
make their own way, darkness was coming on.
A miner Jameson had picked up for guide,
frightened by the Boer fusillade, slipped away,
and they were forced to laager for the night
under a dropping fire. The next morning, at
first light, another guide was procured, who led
the column into the death-trap at Doornkop.

No one in the column knew the way—a
circumstance easily explained by the fact that
everyone travels by rail, and not by road, from
Johannesburg to Krugersdorp.

Resistance was hopeless; for not only were
the men and horses tired out, but they were
enclosed by Boer generalship in a species of
deathtrap, where they were without shelter
from the Krupp guns of the *Staats artillerie*
and the rifle fire of an unseen enemy, now some
thousands strong. It is certain that till nearly

the end Jameson's optimism remained undiminished and he never even contemplated
the possibility of failure. He was within a
few miles of Johannesburg, and till the guide
led them into the sluit there was nothing, he
thought, but open country before him, where
the Boers would not have dared to make a
stand and incur the risk they most dread of a
charge of cavalry.

No one in Johannesburg had the least idea
that Jameson was in difficulties till they received the unbelievable news of his surrender.
There were above twenty thousand stout-
hearted men, many of them hardy Afrikanders
of the Cape Colony and resolute Englishmen,
and though there were arms for only two
thousand five hundred, yet half that number,
led by an officer of Colonel Rhodes's experience, could have easily turned the Boer position
and converted impending defeat into victory.
The fact is, that from the very first the fates
fought against Jameson. From start to finish

he was dragged down by a pitiless chain of adverse circumstances. From the misconduct of the troopers who left uncut the wires that warned Pretoria, down to the incompetency of the guide who led Jameson and his officers out of the right route to their destination, an enterprise of Elizabethan dash and daring was foredoomed to failure.

After the news of Jameson's surrender arrived it was all the Reform leaders could do to hold back their people, who were eager to sally out and attempt a rescue of a popular hero. The Reform leaders were threatened with violence by a crowd of angry and resolute men, because they were unable to serve out the rifles and ammunition, with the supposed existence of which they had "bluffed" the Boers and also necessarily raised the expectations of the citizens. It must always be remembered that one false step had much to do with the attitude of Johannesburg; the Reformers, before they knew of Jameson's unexpected advance, to prevent which they had sent Heany and Holden, had visited Pretoria and entered into an armistice with President Kruger on the basis of promises, made only to be broken, of a concession of a great part of the reforms for which they had taken action.

It is characteristic of Mr. Rhodes's clear and just mind that when all Cape Town, headed by the *Cape Times*, were pouring out their loathing at the miserable cowardice of Johannesburg, he broke silence just as he was leaving for England with a statement which has since been proved to be literally true, "The Uitlanders were no cowards; they were rushed."

CHAPTER IX.

THE news of Jameson's advance came, as we
have seen, upon Mr. Rhodes on Sunday,
December 29th, like a thunderbolt from the
blue. He was, for the time being, over-
whelmed. He foresaw only too clearly all that
followed. He saw himself ruined at the
Cape, and all his plans for the Union of South
Africa fallen in pieces like a house of cards.
" The doctor has ruined us all," was his first
comment; " there, he has ruined him," pointing to a leading Transvaaler at his side. Mr.
Schreiner's evidence in the Cape Blue-Book is
to the same effect. Mr. Rhodes was a different
man; dejected and broken down. " The impression on my mind," says Mr. Schreiner

in his evidence, "is that Mr. Rhodes at the time absolutely disapproved of Jameson going in." He was actually far more concerned for Jameson than for himself; and he seems to have guided his immediate action, especially with regard to the High Commissioner's Proclamation, by a strong feeling of sympathy for his friend which made him anxious to give him every possible chance to avoid the impending failure. A less large and generous nature would have taken care to safeguard himself, but Mr. Rhodes thought only of standing by his impetuous comrade, of not making the situation worse for his old friend by disowning him. "Poor old Jameson," he said to Mr. Schreiner, "twenty years we have been friends, and now he goes in and ruins me. I cannot hinder him; I cannot go and destroy him."

In judging of the various telegrams sent before and after the raid, it must be remembered that Mr. Rhodes habitually delegates all detail work to his secretaries and lieutenants, and is absolutely ignorant of the contents of half of the telegrams ; though at his examination before the Select Committee, he generously took upon himself the responsibility for everything, in order to shield his followers.

As to the situation at Johannesburg, it may be noted that the High Commissioner, who had made every effort to recall Jameson, had also, humbly obedient to the order of Mr. Hofmeyr, the head of the Afrikander Bond, issued a Proclamation, actually dictated by Mr. Hofmeyr, a mere private citizen, repudiating Dr. Jameson, and calling on Her Majesty's subjects at Johannesburg to give him neither support nor encouragement.

This Proclamation undoubtedly was instrumental in paralysing the action of the English at Johannesburg ; for, of course, a British officer like Colonel Rhodes, and even a British subject like Lionel Phillips, felt the difficulty of disobeying an order that plainly commanded them not to help Jameson, and commanded

them to thus desist in the Queen's name.
If the action of the Uitlanders was hampered
before by the Armistice arranged with Pretoria, their hands were tied behind their backs
by the Proclamation. In sending this Proclamation, which endeavoured to deprive them of
their liberty of action, Her Majesty's Government unquestionably assumed a heavy responsibility. The Uitlanders were appealed to, as
subjects of the Queen of England, and commanded on their allegiance not to aid the cause
of their own freedom. They obeyed ; and by
their obedience made the British Government
doubly responsible for their deliverance from
the Boer servitude, from which they were about
to seek deliverance by force of arms. Sir Hercules Robinson went up to Pretoria to plead
with President Kruger, while Sir Jacobus de
Wet failed to carry out the mission personally
to take to Jameson the Queen's order to retire
from the Transvaal territory.

The news that Jameson was defeated and a

prisoner in the hands of the Boers, and would probably be shot, was still convulsing public opinion in London ; when the German Emperor, with characteristic maladroitness, revealed his thinly-veiled intentions upon South Africa in his telegram of congratulation to President Kruger. England received the telegram with a storm of indignation. A flying squadron was at once commissioned, and in an incredibly short time was ready for sea. The Emperor's insult had gained a deeper significance when it was discovered that an intrigue had been going on for some time between Pretoria and Berlin, and that Germany had actually gone so far as to seek from Portugal permission to land marines at Delagoa Bay to send up to the Transvaal. Baron von Marschall had, it appears, on December 30th, already informed the German Consul at Pretoria that German marines were ready to be landed from the Sec-Adler and had notified the German Consulate at Delagoa Bay, that permission had been asked from Portugal for their landing. This intended action of Germany, in contempt of England's suzerainty, was, of course, nothing more than the attempt to redeem at what seemed the psychological moment the pledge of support which was the basis of the long intrigue that had been going on between President Kruger and the **Government at** Berlin—an intrigue which developed rapidly after Dr. Leyds had set about his secret mission at Berlin and his negotiations at Lisbon.

The fact that President Kruger had been for some time exerting himself to give to Germany and the German railway a monopoly of the trade of the Transvaal, did not lessen **the** importance of the latest development of the German Emperor's forward policy in South **Africa.** Thus the ill-fated Jameson raid sank into **its** proper place of merely temporary and accidental minor importance, as simply a blunder of overhaste which had unexpectedly served as a searchlight to reveal the designs of Germany, the disloyalty of the Transvaal Government to its suzerain power, and the danger of the richest and most valuable territory in South Africa becoming not only a menace to the peace of its neighbours, but also a formidable obstacle to the continuance of our hegemony in one of the most important regions of Greater Britain.

While Great Britain was thus rising in its strength to repulse the rivalry of Germany the unhappy English population in Johannesburg, their leaders paralysed by the action of the High Commissioner, were in a position of considerable danger. A large force of Boers with Krupp guns lay outside the town. Jameson and his men had been taken to Pretoria. The men of Johannesburg, furious at the surrender of their ally, which had taken place without their knowledge, within striking distance of their town, were clamouring for arms, threatening the Reform leaders, and demanding to be led to Pretoria to the rescue of Jameson. Had hostilities broken out the Boer artillery could have reduced the town to ruins from the hills that commanded it, while provisions and water could have been cut off and the people starved out. The Reform Committee, therefore, if they had before, like all Committees, shown some lack of decision and initiative, which was not wonderful, their leader and ablest man being absent in Cape Town, undoubtedly showed considerable moral courage and self-abnegation in the attitude they now assumed; for Johannesburg was full of women and children, who must have suffered severely in the event of the investment and bombardment of the town. Sir Hercules Robinson, who was now at Pretoria with President Kruger, sent our agent, Sir Jacobus De Wet, to Johannesburg to induce the Johannesburghers to disarm. President Kruger was under the impression that Johannesburg had 20,000 stand of arms, a corresponding supply of ammunition, and a number of Maxims and field artillery, so successfully had he been "bluffed." Sir Jacobus De Wet urged disarmament in consideration of three concessions. Firstly, that Jameson's life should be spared. Secondly, that the desired reforms should be favourably considered at Pretoria, with a view to grant them. Thirdly, that the Reform leaders should go unpunished, or that, at most, any punishment should be nominal. On these terms the disarmament was effected, but no sooner were the Uitlanders in his power, than President Kruger kept faith by arresting the leaders and throwing them into prison on a charge of High Treason.

The promise of taking into consideration the Uitlanders' grievances was also found to lack fulfilment, and the Reform leaders, after a sojourn in a Boer prison, were tried and sentenced to death. This high-handed contempt of the terms of the disarmament, together with the monstrous nature of the sentence, sent a thrill of horror through South Africa, which reached even to England, and President Kruger very judiciously took care that the sentences should be commuted to fines of £25,000 each for the leaders, which, together with a long and trying imprisonment, proved to be the " nominal " punishment that had been virtually guaranteed by Her Majesty's representative. The other Uitlander leaders were condemned to heavy fines and considerable terms of imprisonment, and, altogether, President Kruger must have obtained about £212,000 in fines, which more than paid any expenses directly caused by the Raid.

The exasperation of the Uitlanders has resulted in a very natural alienation of their regard for Great Britain, which they have to thank for the following benefits :—

First, they loyally responded to the appeal of the Proclamation, and their action to assist their allies was paralyzed. Then they were induced to surrender their arms on terms guaranteed by the British Agent, of which no part was kept, except the promise to spare Jameson's life, and that, before two months were passed, was discovered to have been a gross deception on the part of the Boers, rendered possible by the weakness, due, no doubt, to ill-health, of the High Commissioner; the terms of surrender arranged between Sir John Willoughby on behalf of Jameson's force, and Commandant Cronje on behalf of the Boers, had expressly provided that the lives of Dr. Jameson, his officers and men, should be spared.

The Uitlanders were left with the bitter consciousness that they had been deceived and fooled by their wily old enemy at Pretoria, through the instrumentality of the British Government, which they had too loyally obeyed; for Downing Street, having procured their surrender, abandoned them to the tender mercies of President Kruger and his German and Hollander myrmidons, with an indifference calculated to alienate the

affections of the most loyal colonist in South
Africa.

Meanwhile Mr. Rhodes, who had resigned
his position of Premier, had shut himself up at
Groote Schuur, seemingly crushed under the
pressure of a concatenation of adverse circumstances, which not even his sagaciousness could
have foreseen. He was, of course, accused
everywhere not only of having been connected
with the projected revolution at Johannesburg,
but of having sent in Jameson, and that he had
denied this last charge, was held only to add
the heinousness of the desertion of a friend in
his extremity to the offence of having attempted
to seize the Rand to rehabilitate the bankrupt
finances of the Chartered Company. Naturally,
the greater part of the Cape Dutchmen, led by
Mr. Hofmeyr, took the worst view of the
suspicious circumstances connected with Jameson's raid, and Mr. Hofmeyr himself publicly
and severely condemned the conduct of his old
ally. Mr. Rhodes's purpose was held to be

nothing less than the forcible annexation of the Republic, and the strong racial sympathies of the Dutch in the Cape Colony were played upon and aroused to the utmost on behalf of their countrymen across the Vaal.

Mr. Rhodes, on his way up to Bulawayo, was summoned back by the Chartered Board, and very unwillingly complied. He arrived in England on February 4th, 1896, and after interviews with Mr. Chamberlain and with the Directors of the Chartered Company, found that nothing could be done at the moment. The trials pending at Pretoria and in London made it impossible to speak without harming his friends; and presently, loathing the idea of a long and purposeless stay in London, he started for Rhodesia by way of Beira. He has been severely blamed in the press for not making a clean breast at that time of his connection with Jameson's expedition; but his silence was, if rightly considered, the action of a statesmanlike mind.

Apart altogether from the danger of harming friends on trial by speaking out, he did exactly what Mr. Chamberlain has done under the cloud of similar suspicions, engendered by the vigorous and picturesque, if somewhat sensational, methods of the most prominent exponent of the New Journalism. Mr. Chamberlain has been urged and even entreated to speak out; to make a clean breast of his complicity with the actual raid. He has been even roundly accused of being responsible for the whole thing; " he was in it up to neck." He has kept silence with a proper sense of his dignity, refusing to exculpate himself, and waiting for the proper time and the proper place to offer to the British public a full explanation of his action.

Mr. Rhodes has done exactly the same; and it would not be too much to say that the present Colonial Secretary appears to have followed the example set him by the ex-Cape Premier. Mr. Rhodes has very

properly waited to speak out till the Select
Committee should enter upon the Parliamentary Inquiry. Mr. Chamberlain too has,
with equal propriety, waited till he could give
an account of his position before the same
tribunal.

Mr. Chamberlain, be it remembered, heartily
approved of Mr. Rhodes's line of action, and
publicly praised the wisdom of his hasty return to Rhodesia, where he could give real
aid in the development of the country, though
the services that he was soon to render to
Rhodesia could have been anticipated by no
one—not even by himself.

After Mr. Rhodes had returned to Rhodesia
to devote himself wholly to the development
of that country, which, such was the anger
against him of the Dutch party in Cape
Colony, seemed likely to be the sphere of his
work for some years, the innings of his
enemies began in earnest, and every effort was
made to so misrepresent his motives and his

action and blacken his character as to make it impossible for him to return to public life.

President Kruger and his allies in the English press, ceased not to urge the abrogation of the charter and the punishment of its founder, fearing, with very good reason, that the declaration, " My political life is only just begun," showed that this strong exponent of the Imperial idea was not done with yet. The Trial of the Reformers at Pretoria, of course, involved disclosures of Mr. Rhodes's connection with, and liberal help to, the Reform Movement at Johannesburg, and the Parliamentary Inquiry at the Cape emphasized the main facts of the position, though there it was plainly shown that circumstantial evidence, as well as the evidence of opponents like Mr. Schreiner, exonerated him from the chief charge, the charge of having sent in Dr. Jameson.

The trial of Dr. Jameson, in July, added nothing to what was already known. Dr.

Jameson and his officers, called upon to suffer for their ill-judged but honest patriotism, took their punishment in silence like brave and honourable men.

While Mr. Rhodes's attitude towards Jameson's serious error of judgment has been magnanimous, and that of the Uitlanders in general has been, considering what they have suffered, not altogether lacking in consideration, it has been left to the Lord Chief Justice of England, apparently through fear of foreign opinion and a feeble anxiety to pose as perfectly impartial, to treat the English officers and their gallant leader, when they appeared before him, as though they had been common criminals instead of honourable Englishmen who had merely erred through excess of devotion to the Empire.

It was not the attitude of Mr. Labouchere, whom he regards as at any rate an open, if virulent enemy, but the attitude of the Lord Chief Justice, Lord Russell, that Mr. Rhodes's celebrated phrase of " unctuous rectitude " was

intended to describe. As applied to Lord
Russell's attitude at the trial, where he seemingly forgot that he was not the prosecuting
counsel, and used all **the art** of a great advocate
and all the weight of the highest judicial
position to procure a conviction, Mr. Rhodes's
phrase is admirably true, **and is** not likely
soon to be forgotten.

Mr. Rhodes had long before this placed his
resignation of the position of Managing Director in the hands of the Directors of the Chartered Company. They very properly hesitated
for a long time to accept it, and I am inclined
to think would have been well advised had
they treated the clamour of the hostile press in
London with contempt, and refused to accept
the resignation at all.

In this course they would undoubtedly **have**
had **the** support of the shareholders, who were
perfectly **well** aware that Mr. Rhodes was too
valuable **an asset** to relinquish, for a real and
final severance of its great founder's connec-

tion with it would undoubtedly mean the virtual collapse of that gigantic scheme of colonization and development.

The acceptance of the resignation did not, however, involve such serious consequences; for Mr. Rhodes had given assurances that he would still, in the event of his resignation being accepted, devote himself to the development of Rhodesia, and his friend, Mr. Beit, had promised in the same way to continue his interest and co-operation in the great enterprise with which both of them have now ceased to have any official connection. Of course, the fact that Mr. Rhodes was no longer Managing Director made not the slightest difference in the supremacy which the greatness of his personality and his services had given him among the English and Dutch settlers of Southern Rhodesia.

Earl Grey succeeded Dr. Jameson as the chief official in Rhodesia of the Chartered Company, but highly capable and active as his successful administration showed him to be, there was never for a moment a doubt in the minds of Rhodesians as to who was their real head. The Company might for various reasons change from time to time the person who was their official representative in their dominions, but white man and native alike have refused to recognize any other head than Cecil Rhodes, who found his personality appreciated and understood for itself by his own people in the empire he had carved out for England and civilization from the heart of African savagery.

Probably Mr. Rhodes himself was heartily glad to escape from the boredom of London to the free life of the Veldt and the bright horizons of a young and growing civilization, which had been brought into existence by his exertions, and which was to be successfully brought out of its difficult struggle with the forces of barbarism by the foresight and daring, and at the imminent risk, of its founder and head.

N

CHAPTER X.

MR. RHODES left England in February, 1896, and travelled by way of Egypt and Beira to Mashonaland, his ultimate destination being Bulawayo. His purpose was to devote himself to the development of the country, and primarily to push on the two railway systems, the railway from Beira, which was to connect Salisbury, and Mashonaland in general, with the east coast, advancing by way of Umtali; and the railway, which was to be pushed forward with increased speed, to connect Cape Town, by way of Mafeking and Palapye, with the capital of Matabeleland, Bulawayo.

At Bulawayo, which had rapidly grown into a flourishing town with every characteristic of a high civilization, he proposed to take up his permanent residence, and to throw his unerring business ability and Napoleonic power of inspiring enthusiasm for his far-reaching schemes, into the work of making the vast unoccupied regions of Rhodesia a fit home for English and Dutch families, the largest, the most fertile and most valuable of the possessions of the British Crown in South Africa. The telegraph was to be pushed on northward to Tanganyika with all speed, the railways were to follow; the great belt of highly mineralized country in Southern Rhodesia was to be developed, and although there was no *banket*, and the mine-owner must depend on quartz reefs, yet the richness of the best quartz reefs in the Lydenburg district, such as those of the Transvaal Gold Mining Estates, gave good reason for the expectation that Johannesburg would be vastly surprised at the results, when crushing began in Matabeleland.

The encouragement of pastoral and agricultural development, too, was in Mr. Rhodes's mind, as it has been ever since he personally took Rhodesia in hand, when the extent of the sweet Veldt that would give pasture to innumerable herds and flocks, interested him far more than the promise of the numerous gold-bearing reefs on which work had begun. For Mr. Rhodes looks far beyond the immediate future, beyond the wealth to be extracted from the gold mines. He looks to the permanent value of the country for settlers, and hopes to see it covered with farms and filled with an agricultural population before many years are over. The gold will bring an adventurous population quickly, the excellence of the soil and climate will gradually cover the land with farmsteads from the Limpopo to the Zambesi, and, in due time, when only the great memory of the founder of the State remains with his people, Englishmen and Dutchmen, amalgamated into one nation under the British flag, will cover the healthy northern

plateaux into the very heart of the last unoccupied continent. Revolving schemes of such
far-reaching beneficence for the over-crowded
millions of England, and for the hard-pressed
manufactures of the Mother Country, which
will here find a new and increasingly valuable
market, Mr. Rhodes returned to Rhodesia, and
found much to occupy his attention and demand
his personal presence in the condition of the
colonists in Mashonaland. But his plans of
industrial development were to be rudely
checked, for destiny had marked him out to
serve Rhodesia that same year in other ways
than he had proposed to himself, and in so
serving the country that bears his name, to
reveal himself in his true character to the
Rhodesians and also to all those who are proud
to be called Englishmen.

For some time after Jameson's men were
made prisoners in the Transvaal, peace and
prosperity reigned as before in Matabeleland.
The natives had so long quietly acquiesced in

the new *régime*, that nothing seemed more unlikely than that any serious disturbance should arise. In February, indeed, rumours that the white man's rule was to be overthrown began to be spread abroad among the Matabele. These rumours were traceable to the M'limo, the Makalakas' god who lived in a cave in the Matopo Hills. Shortly before this the rinderpest, coming south with destroying course from Masailand, had crossed the Zambesi and begun its ravages among the cattle of Matabeleland, and this mysterious visitation was turned to account by the ghostly adviser of the natives, whose cave in the Matopos was the Delphi of the whole native population. This voice, speaking from a cave, bears a curious resemblance to the Greek oracle; being a supernatural voice which speaks through a priest, the M'limo, somewhat as the Delphic inspiration did through a priestess, the Pythia. Probably both the Greek and the African oracle got credit for superhuman knowledge by the

same methods as Alexander the impostor **of**
Abonitichos described by Lucian, or the successful spiritualistic medium of modern civilization. This was the first sign of the trouble
that was coming, but it naturally made no impression on the Colonists, who were too much
occupied with the advance of the rinderpest to
foresee any other calamity.

It was not till the latter part of March that
the rebellion actually broke out. It began
with an attack on the native police, and was
immediately followed up by the massacre of the
whites, the men, women, and children scattered
over the country at farms and mines, and unsuspecting and defenceless. It was the wanton
cruelty of this merciless slaughter of women and
children that gave a bitterness to the fighting
which had been unknown in the War of Conquest in 1893. Murders took place almost
simultaneously all over the country. When
the news reached Bulawayo the colonists at
once flew to arms. The Hon. Maurice Gifford

at once turned out with forty men, and relieved about thirty whites who had laagered at Cumming's Store. Here a fierce attack by the Matabele, which was beaten off with some difficulty, showed that the blacks meant business. Gifford, with a soldier's instinct, at once perceived this, and, in a letter to Napier, predicted what followed. "This, in my opinion, will prove a more serious business than the old war."

The insurrection of the Matabele found the settlers leaderless and unprepared. The Indunas were at its head, and the whole Matabele race, with a few exceptions, threw themselves into the enterprise. There were forty-eight mounted white police in the country, but half the native police with their rifles joined the rebels, and the rest had to be disarmed. Jameson had left over 1,000 Lee-Metfords and some Martinis, with about a million rounds of ammunition; but there were only 800 men to use them. The rest of the men in Matabeleland were besieged at the various laagers and therefore could not be employed on the offensive.

It is not my purpose to record at length the exploits of the Colonists, the gallant conduct of the early campaign by Gifford and the other leaders, the admirable spirit of the men, and the way in which the Rhodesians on every occasion showed themselves able to maintain the honour of the British name, and, remembering the Afrikander corps, one must not forget to add, of the Dutch. What death could have been worthier a brave man than Baxter's, of Grey's Scouts, who was surrounded and killed at the Umguza, after he had given up his horse to a wounded comrade, whose life he thus saved at the expense of his own? What action pluckier than Lieutenant Crewe's, who also gave up his horse to the wounded Lieutenant Hook, and fought his way out of the pursuing Kaffirs on foot?

In short, the Matabele insurrection has

given the Rhodesians the opportunity of showing of what splendid stuff they are made,
though this has been their record since
Wilson's men, refusing to leave their wounded,
made their last stand on the Shangani River
in 1893. The same spirit that animated the
attacking columns of Colonists in Matabeleland was found in Mashonaland in such a
gallant rescue against great odds as the
relief of the women, who were brought off safe
to Salisbury from the Alice Mine through
swarms of natives and under a continual and
deadly fusillade.

It was a little after the middle of May,
1896, when Mr. Rhodes, with Sir Charles
Metcalfe and others, came into Matabeleland
with the Salisbury relief force from Mashonaland. There they joined Colonel Napier's
column from Bulawayo, which had come to
meet them, and were soon in the thick of the
fighting. Finding the kraals of the natives
full of white men's loot, and the crops and

stores all intact, they perceived at once that the Matabele thought they **had** finally driven the white men out of **this** part of the country.

It was determined to endeavour to bring the rebels to bay, and the discovery of the remains of English and Dutch women and children who had been treacherously murdered made the men of this patrol along the Insiza River eager to carry out Mr. Rhodes's **advice,** and **give the** bloodthirsty savages **"an** ever-lasting lesson." Though **Mr.** Rhodes, **with** Van Rensburg **and** Selous, **was** anxious to begin at once, there was some delay on the part of the commanding officer in getting to work ; but once they reached the neighbour-hood of the Insiza River there was plenty of fighting to do, though thick bush prevented the white men getting to close quarters. After his arrival at Bulawayo Mr. Rhodes, on June 5th, accompanied McFarlane's patrol to the Umguza, where he took part in some heavy fighting. At the fighting at Shiloh at a later date Mr. Rhodes, riding ahead of the column, escaped by a miracle from a sudden volley from the bush at only thirty paces distance, and set, as he did throughout, an example of imperturbable coolness and courage. At Thabas-i-Mamba again he was conspicuous where the fight was sharpest; and it was in vain that he was entreated not to expose a life of such supreme importance to the whole community in Rhodesia.

After the arrival of Sir Frederick Carring-ton to take the command, the disbandment of the Bulawayo field-force took place on July 4th, and the remainder of the work of crushing the rebellion was left to the Imperial troops. The rebels had gathered in strength in the Matoppos, and Colonel Plumer and Lieu-tenant-Colonel Baden-Powell undertook the task of dislodging them. The attack on Si-kombo's mountain, where Major Kershaw and Captain Hervey lost their lives, and several officers and men were wounded, was only one of a series of engagements in which the loss of the troops was heavy. Between the 20th of July and the 5th of August, 1896, the column lost 200 killed and wounded, out of a strength of 1,000. It became perfectly plain, both to the officers in command and everyone else, that the whole available force was quite too small to continue the exceedingly costly work of carrying position after position in the Matopos.

A much larger force of men—at least 5,000 Imperial troops — would be required to dislodge the rebel Indunas from their fastnesses in the hills. There was no hope of ending the war the same year. All the troops at the disposal of General Carrington could do was to drive the rebels from kopje to kopje, and even this could not be continued at the heavy cost of the last four engagements. There was nothing for it but for General Carrington to go into winter quarters in Bulawayo, being 500 miles from his base and without any transport service owing to the ravages of the rinderpest.

An Imperial force of sufficient strength for the work could, then, be sent up in 1897.

This programme was the only one possible in the opinion of the commanding officer. Mr. Rhodes saw that this was too true; and he also perceived that it would cost at least five millions to the Chartered Company to bring the war to a close in this way. This would mean ruin to the Company, coming on the top of their other extraordinary expenses.

The period of the Proclamation had been extended, but the rebels had practically held their own in the Matopos, and there was not the slightest chance of their accepting a pardon from which all the leading Indunas were excluded. The Indunas, according to the Proclamation of Sir R. Martin, were to come down to Bulawayo and be tried for their lives; an invitation that, backed by their well-armed impis, they were not very likely to accept. The future of the Chartered Company, the future of Rhodesia, depended on bringing the war to an immediate end. Then it was that **Mr. Rhodes** found scope and play for **the high qualities that underlie** the **massive strength of his personality.** **A great** occasion found **the** man to use it. General Carrington's troops, with all the gallant leading of the officers, and the plucky following of the men, had failed **at the impossible** task set them. Mr. Rhodes himself, unaided, undertook to bring the war to an end, and obtained from General Carrington **permission to** enter upon the apparently desperate venture.

The motive that actuated Mr. Rhodes was a strong one; the fate of Rhodesia was in the balance, and his proposed action was nothing less than to go, unguarded and unarmed, to meet **the** Matabele Indunas, and, if possible, induce them to accept his terms and end **the** war.

CHAPTER XI.

THE PACIFICATION OF MATABELELAND.

MR. RHODES's first step was to move his camp away from the troops and up to the foot-hills of the Matopos. There he lay, in an unguarded camp, within striking distance of the Matabele impis. Any night the camp could have been rushed and Mr. Rhodes taken prisoner or killed, which, as the natives one and all regarded him as the king of the white men, was a not improbable contingency. It was not from mere daring that Mr. Rhodes took this risk, but from the definite purpose of inspiring trust in the rebel Indunas as to his peaceable disposition towards them. The result justified his sagacity, and came up to his expectations.

About noon one day (I condense from the report of Captain Stent, the special correspondent of the *Cape Times*, and add some local colour obtained from another of those present) John Grootboom, the Xosa Kaffir, distinguished for his pluck in the two Matabele wars, came from the Matopos into Rhodes's camp, and informed the white men that a great Indaba, or Council, had been called together in the depths of the Matopos a few miles away. The Indunas did not dare to come down into the open because of the white soldiers, but they wished to see Johann, their old friend. Mr. Johan Colenbrander, a wonderfully patient and successful interpreter, knows the native character and the native languages better, probably, than any other white man living. Colenbrander might well be called an old friend by the Matabele, inasmuch as he had come to London with Lobengula's Indunas, as interpreter and guide, in 1889, and one of those Indunas, Babyaan, was now a chief among the rebels.

o

The rebel Indunas scarcely dared to hope that Mr. Rhodes would come, but if he would come to the Council he would, they said, be welcome.

This was just the opportunity Mr. Rhodes desired, and he seized it without hesitation. He took with him Colenbrander as interpreter, Dr. Hans Sauer, and Captain Stent, the correspondent, on whose account, added to that of another member of the party, my narrative is based. Two natives, John Grootboom and Makunga, accompanied the four white men. Three of the whites carried revolvers in their pockets. Mr. Rhodes carried nothing but a switch, a habit of his when in danger or under fire, which reminds one of the fatalism of his old friend Gordon, who in the Chinese War carried nothing but a cane. The path led up into the Matopos, winding among the granite kopjes and boulders. By a narrow gorge, through the granite hills, they made their way past kopjes and thick bushy scrub that would have afforded excellent cover for an ambush.

They all knew the danger—none better than
Mr. Rhodes, whose restless, nervous energy
made him conscious of every detail of his surroundings. At last, through the neck of a
narrow gorge, their horses picked their way
into a small amphitheatre, somewhat resembling a *cirque* in the Pyrenees, enclosed on
all sides by lofty walls of granite rock, many
hundreds of feet in height, and dominated by a
huge granite kopje. The kopje and the heights
were alive with armed Matabele warriors,
whose heads peeped out, showing like black
balls against the grey granite, from the shelter
of the crevices and boulders, as they looked
down on the little party of defenceless white
men below.

Mr. Rhodes halted his horse in a mealie
patch and dismounted. His companions
followed his example. The decisive moment
had come. Was it a stratagem of the savages
to get the great white chief into their power,
or was it in good faith that the invitation to
the Indaba had been given? Did the natives

desire to lay their grievances before him whom
they regarded as the king of the white men,
or did they merely wish by a ruse not unknown
in savage warfare to deprive the whites of
their chief? The question was soon decided.
The white men had not long dismounted when
a white flag flashed from the kopje, and a
long array of Matabele Indunas followed in
single file, and, fixing the flag in the ground,
sat down in a half-moon formation round the
four white men. The natives were Indunas
of age and weight in the nation. Nearly all
wore on their heads the ring, the distinguishing mark of responsible warriors. I remember
observing with some curiosity this ring on one
of these very Indunas, a good many years ago.
Among them were Sikombo, Babyaan, Umlu-
gulu, a man of great importance in Lobengula's
time, and some consider a chief instigator of
the rebellion, Dhliso, and other leaders of the
Matabele. Mr. Rhodes, who sat some way
up on the side of an antheap, greeted them in

Zulu, "You are well out of it." The Indunas responded with the same good wish for the white chief and his Indunas. Then there was a long pause. Mr. Rhodes told Colenbrander to ask them to come to business. Colenbrander said, "Tell your troubles to Rhodes, your father. He has come among you unarmed, with peace in his heart." Then first one Induna, and after him another, waxed eloquent with their complaints. The chief of these complaints was the misconduct of the native police. The young men, their sons and servants, went (said they) to Bulawayo, enlisted in the police, and then returned, and, rifle in hand, lorded it over their own fathers, beat them, raped their women, seized their cattle, and there was no redress to be obtained. Mr. Rhodes assured them that there were to be no more native police. Satisfied on this head, they next complained of the native Commissioners who, they said, had taken their women, for whom they had paid twenty cows,

and given them to their own men. The difficulty of the cattle, too, was brought forward.
The Administrator had, they said, promised
that only the King's cattle should be taken, and
that each man should keep his own; this had
not been done. The rinderpest, Mr. Rhodes
pointed out, had settled that question and
killed all.

At last Mr. Rhodes stopped their complaints
by sternly advancing the most serious charge
he had against them. "I am not angry with
you for fighting us, but why did you kill our
women and children? For this you deserve no
forgiveness." It was, as Mr. Colenbrander
warned Mr. Rhodes, dangerous criticism in
such a place—an unarmed white man boldly
accusing the chiefs of the Matabele nation of
their worst wrongdoing, while crowds of
armed warriors looked on from the kopjes and
boulders around, and the lifting of a hand
would have brought them down like wolves
on their prey.

Then Mr. Rhodes, impatient at the long discussion of non-essentials, came to the point. " All this is of the past," he said (Colenbrander translated for him throughout). " Now for the future.   Is it peace or is it war ? "

One of the Indunas at once took up a stick and held it above his head.   Then, throwing it down at the feet of Mr. Rhodes, he cried, " See ! this is my gun ; I throw it down at your feet.   This is my assegai," repeating the action ; and all the Indunas loudly assented.

Then Mr. Rhodes explained the situation. The cattle were all dead.   The time for sowing had come ; the rain was at hand.   Let there be peace now, or they would have famine soon. To this argument he added the assurance, " I will remain with you in the land, and you can come to me with your troubles."   This promise was received with encouraging applause.

Then the Induna Somnavulu summed up : " It is good, my father, you have trusted us, and we have spoken.   We are all here to-day, and our voice is the voice of the nation We are the mouths and ears of the people. We give you one word. It is peace. The war is over. Your road to Tuli is safe. Try it. We do not break our word. We have spoken." The Council had lasted more than four hours; and the sun was slanting low on the kopjes when Mr. Rhodes, by rising, gave the sign that it was over.

Then came another moment of suspense, not indeed to Mr. Rhodes, who felt that he had won. The natives crowded in on the whites, entreating for tobacco, which was given them, and down from the kopjes well-armed young warriors began to stream into the amphitheatre. The horses stood close by, and Mr. Rhodes's horse had caught its feet in the reins. But anxious not to break the spell by any hasty movement, he waited till his party were ready to start. Then, while the Indunas, with lifted right hands, shouted, " Farewell, Father and King;" Mr. Rhodes turned his horse's head and made his way slowly back to camp, conscious that the big work he had set himself was done, that the Chartered Company was safe, and Rhodesia delivered.

Thus was an enterprise of great pith and moment greatly carried through. Dull must be the imagination which cannot picture to itself the grandeur of this scene, where one of England's Worthies comes unarmed and un-guarded into the lair of a savage race, at bay, well-armed and desperate, and overawes them by his perfect fearlessness and dignity, and wins them by his fairness and generosity. "One of those scenes in life which make it worth living," was the comment of the hero of the scene him-self as he rode away. The peace thus won for Rhodesia proved, as Mr. Rhodes was convinced it would, to be permanent. The Indunas kept their word, and the Matabele loyalty to the chiefs is of more than feudal firmness.

Every detail of this Indaba is worth observing. It is a convincing proof of the sterling metal of which the manhood of the Great Man of South Africa is made. It is also a valuable illustration of his method of dealing with the natives. Wise and tactful because sympathetic, patient and humane, Mr. Rhodes treats the Kaffirs as men, reasons with them as a man with men, shows that he believes in the potentialities of a common humanity by expecting his trust of them to make them trust him. A valuable object lesson of the proper relations between white man and black, which might be studied with advantage by Mrs. Cronwright-Schreiner.

After this Mr. Rhodes remained for weeks in his camp by the Matopos, unguarded and unarmed; and every day, and at all hours of the day, he was open to the visits of any of the Indunas who chose to come to him. They used to send no notice of their coming, but simply walk in and sit down on the ground and talk with him about their own prospects and intentions, and the method in which they were

to be ruled for the future.   At these informal
palavers Mr. Rhodes used genially to chaff the
Indunas and point out to them how easily they
could send their young men down any night and
kill him.   Then the Indunas would be quite
hurt and would entreat him not to put upon
them the mere suspicion of such bad faith.
Thus gradually he completely won their confidence and liking.   He got to know them, and
they got to know him personally, till at last
they used to sleep at his camp, and finally
fetched their wives out of the hills, all their
doubts and suspicions having melted away.
The wise and humane attitude of the great
white chief produced the natural effect; for
one of the complaints against the officials had
been that they treated the Indunas with open
contempt.   Sikombo, for instance, complained
that when he went to Bulawayo and had asked
for meat he had been told by the white men to
go and eat his dogs, and he thought it better
to die than endure such an insult.

With untiring patience, tact, and kindliness, Mr. Rhodes stayed on in his camp by the fastnesses of the rebels till they had been accustomed to come and consult him about everything as their father and friend; and the knowledge that he would live in the country and see that they were fairly treated undoubtedly contributed largely to the final peace that has been established in Matabeleland.

Mr. Rhodes's words to the Indunas at the close of the last Indaba at his camp before he left for Bulawayo are a summary of his action and his policy: "Johann and I have now lived two months among you. I was advised to fear you and live among the White Impis. I said, 'No, I will live among my children, and carry no arms in my hand.' We look to you to be good, and we will forget the past. The Indunas must prove their loyalty. I do not believe they will fight again." Here there were loud cries of " Chief and Father," "It is all right, Father." With reason do they

regard him as the great peacemaker and pictur-
esquely describe him as "the bull that separates
the fighting bulls," by which name he is known
throughout Matabeleland.

The arrangement made at this last *Indaba*,
at Mr. Rhodes's camp, by Earl Grey, acting
officially for the Company, ensures, by its
statesmanlike agreement with the Indunas,
the peace of the country. The Indunas are
now salaried officials of the Company, responsible for the behaviour of the people, but under
the control in each district of a white man as
Native Commissioner. Receiving £60 a year
and a horse to ride, each Induna will be careful
to restrain his young men and anxious to
supply the requisite labour for the farms and
the mines; while the excellent wages paid
to native labourers, the influence of regular
work and the growth of the needs of civilization will gradually establish the reign of Industrialism, and more effectually pacify the
country than any disarmament, because the

gradual decay of the old military spirit is the one sure guarantee of permanent peace. Without costing more than an inconsiderable fraction of the expense of the native police, the arrangement made through Earl Grey will guard against the frequent misuse of authority of which a native police is only too likely to be guilty, when away from the white man's supervision.

Thus the Matabele rebellion has ended in a permanent and satisfactory peace, and order and settled government will be established on firm foundations. Black labour is essential to the development of the country, and the habit of work to the general elevation of the black men themselves to a higher stage of development. It may be well to remind Exeter Hall theorists, who criticize this arrangement and would like to break up tribal rule, of the wise words of Wallace, the greatest living authority on the doctrine of evolution :—

"There are certain stages through which society must pass in its onward march from barbarism to civilization. Now one of these stages has always been some form or other of despotism, such as feudalism or servitude, or a despotic paternal government; and we have every reason to believe that it is not possible for humanity to leap over this transition epoch, and pass at once from pure savagery to free civilization."

The blacks are simply overgrown children, and at their inferior stage of development a paternal despotism is the rule best suited to them; which fact, moreover, they recognize themselves. Mr. Rhodes's plan of ending the rebellion, and arranging for native good conduct in the future, has been good for the Chartered Company, which he has saved from the intolerable load of the millions, which would have been required, had it been left to the Imperial troops to finally subdue the Matabele by force. The Matabele have had a lasting lesson; they have learned that even when armed with the white man's weapons they are no match for the white man. The results of Mr. Rhodes's negotiations prove they had had sufficient punishment already.

Mr. Rhodes's policy has been good for the natives also, whom it has saved from further rough handling by the troops, while the rebels would certainly have had to suffer very severely afterwards had the Imperial instructions been carried out. It has been good for the colonists, to whom it has secured in a rational manner the native labour absolutely necessary for the development and progress of the country, while the example he has set by his patient and humane treatment of the natives is invaluable in a community subject to the temptations of the white community in Rhodesia.

At this point it may be well to consider briefly the causes of the rebellion; which have been very commonly set down to the removal of the white police to the Transvaal border by Dr. Jameson, that is to the fault of

Mr. Rhodes and the Chartered Company. The withdrawal of the police was no doubt contributory to the revolt, in that it gave encouragement to waverers; but that withdrawal had taken place months before the rebellion broke out, and to make it the chief cause of the rebellion is merely to furnish a fresh example of an old fallacy. The truth is, the rebellion had been long planned and organised. It sprang primarily from the dislike of a warlike people, accustomed to live by fighting and rapine, to the peaceful life they were obliged to lead. They had never been completely conquered or disarmed. Beaten by rifle and machine-gun fire in two decisive engagements, they had acquiesced in the downfall of Lobengula, since it was followed by his death. They did not like the labour required of them, no doubt, but this alone was insufficient to cause general discontent, and natives from whom no labour was required were foremost in the rising. The

Indunas and the relations of Lobengula were at the bottom of the rebellion, which was nothing less than a bold attempt on their part to reconquer their country and exterminate or expel the white men. The large amount of ammunition possessed, as well as the excellent rifles used by the rebel impis, shows that the preparation for the rebellion must have been going on for a very long time.

A contributory cause of the discontent was, no doubt, the misconduct of the native police, who acted with all the old Matabele swagger and lawlessness in the kraals of their own people. Another, and far more important contributory cause was the rinderpest and the slaughter of the cattle, carried out by the white men in order to prevent the spread of the disease. His cattle are the Matabele's whole wealth; he reckons the price of a woman or a gun at so many cows, and the slaughter of his herd was naturally looked upon by the native in Matabeleland, as since then in Bechuanaland and elsewhere, as a wanton attempt to ruin him; for the real purpose of such measures is completely beyond his comprehension.

But the first and most important cause of the rebellion, sufficient to account for it, had all the lesser causes been wanting, was the resolve of a proud people, who had always lorded it over the other native races, not to submit finally to the rule of the white man (for whom, no doubt, familiarity had not, in many cases, increased their respect), without a bold bid for mastery; and this resolve the influence of the witch doctors, who were heavy losers by the establishment of British civilisation, did much to fan into a flame.

From this cause, soon or late, the rebellion must have come. This is the opinion of all experienced Colonists in Rhodesia. Mr. Rhodes and the Chartered Company are therefore in no sense the cause of the insurrection, though they have given compensation for all losses in the handsomest possible fashion, and actually satisfied the Colonists by the largeness of their generosity.

As for the seriousness of the insurrection, we have ample evidence from the commanding officers of the Imperial troops. Sir Frederick Carrington, for instance, a veteran in African fighting, has put it on record that "in the Matabele Campaign we had fighting of the very first class—the Matabele were splendidly armed. They had ammunition, too, of faultless quality. They fought well, and it was a tough business. Both British troops and Colonials did well." This testimony is worth remembering, as showing what sort of fighting men were the settlers who, up to the arrival of the Imperial troops, successfully dealt with the Matabele impis in many a well-fought engagement. The fighting that to Sir Frederick Carrington appears to be of the very first class, appears to the gallant and veracious Mr.

Labouchere to be exactly like the slaughter of tame pheasants at a battue.

As for Mr. Rhodes's deed of daring, Sir F. Carrington's evidence is worth remembering— the judgment of a brave soldier on a brave civilian. "It was a most plucky thing of Mr. Rhodes to go into the Matopos for a parley with the chiefs to make peace."

It may be worth adding that the suppression of the rebellion was conducted with remarkable moderation, when one considers the intense feeling aroused by the brutal murders, not only of unarmed white men, but also of helpless women and children—murders to the merciless cruelty of which an element of the basest treachery was frequently super-added by the fact that the murdered men and women were often, up to the moment of their slaughter, on the most friendly terms with their murderers.

The spirit of vengeance that was aroused in English soldiers and officers by similar conduct on the part of Sepoys in the Indian mutiny was, of course, present in the settlers of Rhodesia, and it would be to expect almost superhuman virtue in ordinary men to suppose that it should have been absent. This spirit, however, found its expression in the battle-field, and the worst that can be said is that quarter was not given to the beaten Matabele, by whom certainly it was never expected. The after vengeance, however, of a general hanging assizes, when the war was over, was fortunately avoided by the humane and for-giving terms of peace arranged by Mr. Rhodes. "All that is of the past" was the principle he laid down at the fateful Indaba in the Matopos, and he used his great influence to overcome a strong and influential opposition, and to make sure that this principle was acted upon. The Matabele are perfectly well aware to whose clemency they owe their lives, and the rebel Indunas especially have good reasons to be thankful that it was the counsels of Mr. Rhodes, and not the hanging orders of Sir Richard Martin, that prevailed in the end.

I venture to think that this policy of Mr. Rhodes will, in spite of the vaticinations of the advocates of sterner measures, prove to be the wiser, as it is certainly the more humane, course, and it will be interesting to see if this clemency is taken as a sign of weakness by the chiefs, who have seen for themselves in the heart of the Matopos the high and steadfast courage of the great maker and pacificator of Rhodesia.

CHAPTER XII.

WHEN Mr. Rhodes left London in February, 1896, to take up his residence in Rhodesia, he merely carried out the plan he had formed on resigning the Premiership. Even if the rebellion had not broken out in Matabeleland and given him the unexpected opportunity of showing his great qualities in action, and proving to the world of what stuff our foremost pioneer of Empire is made, the presence of its founder and head in Rhodesia was the one thing necessary to encourage and organize the efforts of the Colonists for the development of the country.

As events proved, the presence of Mr. Rhodes during the rebellion was nothing short of a Godsend to the community. His cheery optimism in the midst of difficulties was contagious and heartened the despondent, while it confirmed the faith of the sturdier Colonists in the result of the war, as well as in the future of their adopted land. He insisted on sharing with his fellow Colonists the dangers of the fighting and the discomforts of the campaign. "You must not think," said Mr. Rhodes, speaking afterwards at Bulawayo, "that I incurred unnecessary risk in proceeding with the columns you have sent into the field; but I thought that by going with them I should get a knowledge of the people and a knowledge of the country, and I should share with the people their risks and their responsibilities."

The result to him of being thus closely brought into contact with the Colonists of Rhodesia has been that they, like the Cape Dutchmen, have felt the charm of greatness of ideas combined with simplicity of tastes;

have come to know his large nature and perfect frankness and manliness; and men who once believed in Rhodes from their belief in Jameson, now know their great man and believe in him for himself. The free unconventional life of a young country suited one who needs no trappings of office or title to enhance his greatness, who loves reality and hates ceremony or show.

"So far as I am personally concerned, I have been a happy man since I have been amongst you," was his own testimony at Bulawayo; and "The great secret of life is work," was in Rhodesia, as it had been elsewhere, the ruling principle of his existence. This saved him from looking back at the troubles of the earlier part of the year. His habit of looking forward far ahead no doubt cheered him ; for he saw at the end of a year or two the railways running into Bulawayo and Salisbury, and the speed of Rhodesia's development raised to the nth power. Truly, if the philosopher be right who defined happiness as the free exercise of the higher faculties of a man's nature, Mr. Rhodes in Rhodesia was, as he described himself, a happy man.

All his troubles, however, were not yet over. He had still to go home and be examined before the Select Committee of the House at Westminster. He decided to leave Rhodesia by Beira in order to visit Salisbury and arrange about the railroad to that town by way of Umtali. Sir Charles Metcalfe, the able constructor-in-chief of the railways into Rhodesia, who was with him throughout the insurrection, accompanied him; and on the way Umtali was visited and the completion of the Mashonaland railroad from the East Coast was satisfactorily arranged.

The next question to be decided was whether he should return by the Cape or not. Against the Cape route was the fact that all his old friends, the political leaders, especially Mr. Hofmeyr, were bitterly set against him, and would keenly resent his return to the Cape Colony. Moreover, the large Dutch population ruled by the Afrikander Bond, of which Mr. Hofmeyr is the all-powerful wire-puller, might be expected to receive him not only with coldness, but with open hostility.

It is not pleasant to come, a culprit condemned by public opinion, to the scene of your former popularity and power, even if the condemnation has been the result of flagrant misrepresentation and complete misunderstanding. But whatever quality Mr. Rhodes lacks, he certainly does not lack moral courage. To face the music, to take the bull by the horns, is his way. So in spite of the advice of friends, he elected to go back by the Cape. The best that could be hoped was that he would be allowed to go, without hostile demonstration, quietly back to Cape Town. There the large English population made the Great Imperialist certain of a warm welcome, which was already being planned with remarkable spontaneity, though not without some feeble opposition from a few politicians—individuals who have no followers —such as Mr. Merriman, an advocate of Dutch and German supremacy as far away as Sir Bartle Frere's time, Mr. J. W. Sauer, whose constituents have passed a vote of want of confidence in him for his anti-Rhodes policy, and Mr. Rose Innes, the leader of the Opposition.

The steamer from Beira stayed a few hours at Durban, but Natal, though the population is English, has been forced to surrender to President Kruger's railway policy, and in order to secure a share of the Johannesburg traffic has virtually to take its cue from Pretoria. The townspeople of Durban, however, could not be prevented from giving their distinguished visitor an English welcome, though he refused to be made the object of any formal demonstration.

The reception at Port Elizabeth was another matter. Here he was in his own Cape Colony, and the Cape Colony Englishmen are solid for the representation of English progress and English freedom. A great reception with immense crowds awaited his arrival. Forty old Rhodesians horsed the carriage and drew Mr. Rhodes to the Town Hall.

At the luncheon Mr. Rhodes, who was completely taken by surprise by the enthusiasm of his reception, was forced to speak on the spur of the moment without any preparation. He spoke at great length, however, having first explained that as he was without a speech, he must tell them simply the thoughts that were uppermost in his mind. The result was that the history of the inception of the scheme of Empire to the North was given in detail, and the consequences that have already followed and are to follow with the railways. Mr. Rhodes is something far better than a skilled rhetorician—he is, at his best, full of his subject, intensely in earnest, and his undesigned use of homely similes and familiar colloquialisms aids the effect, while the immense energy of the man flashes forth carrying home his own convictions to the minds of his hearers.

Perhaps the most significant portion of a speech of great sincerity and power—of course not free from the verbal errors of the reporters —was the following passage :—

"You will be surprised to know that, in addition to the large numbers there (*i.e.* in Rhodesia) from the Cape, we have a large number from the Free State. President Kruger's country has sent one thousand human beings there. I have been fighting in company with them lately, and I know no more loyal citizens in the North than those who have come from the Transvaal. It is a pure question of business. They have discovered that there is sweet veldt in the North and sour veldt in the Transvaal. I will venture to make the remark that before half-a-century has passed away we in the North shall have the major portion of the Burghers of the Transvaal. I know of none of the thousands of men, women, and children more loyal to the country, more willing to take a share in the responsibilities of government, than the Burghers from the Transvaal. I do not think the high individual in the Transvaal who a year ago addressed lamentations to the Burghers, warning them they. must not trek into this country, was aware that there was sweet veldt there. . . . There are a very large number in the Administration of young men from the Cape Colony. One of the grievances of Queenstown, I believe, is that we have taken all their young men. . . . Natal sent a contingent to fight the natives, and a large number were desirous of remaining. So one of those curious things is happening. There is a Union of States occurring in the North. I have done my best in my unofficial capacity to promote it, because there are ramifications. Every one who comes there has the impulse to write to his friends and relations, and the relatives find the politicians, and so it all works out. In the North there is no consideration shown for the men of one State as against another, and that means really the Union of Africa. I am told I have promoted great disunion. That may be for the moment. We will leave that question for the future. The question of race never occurred to my mind. Practical proof of that is that, in my social life, the majority of my friends— people on the Diamond Fields and in Cape Town—were men of a race other than English. It is not a question of race. It is a question whether we are to be united or otherwise."

At a later period in his speech he thus laid down his programme : " I don't propose to close my public career, and I am still determined to strive for the closer union of South Africa " ; and to this he added the practical advice : " Base your votes on the higher platform, and attempt to attain closer union, cultivate friendly relations with all you meet, entirely irrespective of race; but state boldly that you will have no foreign interference in this country. In another twenty-five years, I think, if people will take that thought home with them, all will be well."

The dominant notes of this speech, his resolve to return to public life at the Cape, and his principle of South African Union, worked out firstly in Rhodesia and based on the dismissal of all race feeling, run through the numerous speeches which he was obliged to deliver in what soon, to the astonishment of himself and every one else, developed into a veritable triumphal progress, not only in the English districts but in those chiefly or wholly Dutch. As the train ran through the Great Karroo, the scattered population of farmers had collected to greet him at the stations, and, of course, at Kimberley, his own city, he was received enthusiastically. So anxious was he to escape demonstrations that here, where every one was with him and his will is law, his will prevailed, and there was no regular reception.

The really astonishing fact, however, was the reception in the Western Province, the great Dutch centre, the home of the Afrikander Bond. Contrary to every one's expectation, the Dutchmen turned out in large numbers, and at **every** station gave their old friend visible and **audible proof that he was** not only forgiven, but welcomed back with unimpaired confidence.

This country, which is the centre of Mr. Hofmeyr's organisation and influence, put it beyond question that it welcomed back Mr. Rhodes to political life. Mr. Rhodes's announcement that he proposed to return to his seat in Cape Town was received with loud cheers. The signatures of the address **at** Wellington, **as of** the **other** addresses presented at stopping-places in this district, were chiefly Dutch.

Mr. Rhodes, in his reply to the address, referred again to the question of race-feeling. His staunchest friends belonged, he said, "to the race which most of you represent here; and therefore, when at times some of my conduct, when criticized, has been referred to the question of race, **I hope** you know well how perfectly false that is." "I will give you one promise in return, and that promise is, that I am not going out of public life."

At the Paarl five hundred residents received the ex-Premier, and an address was presented, signed by four hundred representative farmers, mostly Dutch. Mr. Rhodes, in the course of his speech, gave the promise that he would retain his seat in the Cape Assembly, and work, not only for the development of the North, but for the closer union of the various elements in South Africa.

These hearty receptions in the strongholds of the Afrikander Bond are far more significant than the more striking spectacle of the great reception at Cape Town, with its address with ten thousand signatures, with its torchlight procession, its immense crowds and unbounded enthusiasm; for in Cape Town the population is mainly English, and naturally enough almost went wild with excitement in welcoming back the greatest Englishman in South Africa, a Cape Colonist like themselves.

It is not for nothing that for years past Mr. Rhodes has laid before the Dutch of the Colony his political ideals; his policy of commercial union, union of interests, looks very bright to them beside President Kruger's policy of isolation with the huge hostile tariff he levies on the products of the hapless Cape farmer on their way to the Johannesburg market.

And so Mr. Hofmeyr's counter demonstrations have fallen very flat, even at the Paarl, and in spite of his own great abilities and the admirable organisation of his caucus, the Afrikander Bond has failed to show that it can carry one-half of the Dutch with it against Mr. Rhodes. At the Paarl, for example, more resident Dutchmen voluntarily signed the address welcoming back Mr. Rhodes, than Mr. Hofmeyr and all the power of the Afrikander Bond could collect together at the opposition meeting, though they had plenty of time for preparation, and though Mr. Hofmeyr is unrivalled in the art of wire-pulling.

The Dutch reaction in favour of Mr. Rhodes is so unmistakably genuine, and the Cape Englishmen are so solid in their support, that if a plebiscite of the Cape Colony were taken to-morrow for the Premiership, there can be no doubt he would be once more the responsible Minister in the Legislative Assembly.

There are plenty of signs how the wind blows, of which one, by no means the least significant, is the open conversion of the quick-witted Sir J. Sivewright to friendlier and saner views than he had previously upheld. He has perceived that Mr. Rhodes will return to power, and he has taken anticipatory steps towards a reconciliation.

Not the least remarkable thing about the remarkable return of the Cape Dutch to their allegiance to Mr. Rhodes, who has also won the solid support of the English, is the fact that in the time when his fortunes were at their nadir, early last year, when even his friends were counselling his retirement from public life, and his enemies eagerly hounding him down, he declared, with his extraordinary insight into the future, that his political life, far from being over, had only just begun.

The event has justified his self-confidence, his prophecy has come true sooner than he himself expected, and he will shortly return to office at the Cape a greater personage in politics than he has ever been before. Mr. Rhodes, then, has won back the more intelligent Dutchmen of the Colony, in part because of their material interests, seriously injured by their fellow Dutchman, the advocate of a narrow and exclusive Dutch supremacy at Pretoria, but chiefly, I think, because they have come to feel they have been unjust to him.

The South African Dutchman is suspicious, but he does not easily remove his trust from one in whom he has reposed it. The Dutch members had learned to know and trust Mr. Rhodes completely; they liked him personally; they liked his large, loose, unconventional ways; his big, frank, independent nature. Their indignation was hot at the time of Jameson's inroad, at what appeared to be an attempt to seize the Transvaal and impose the direct Imperial rule. They began, I think, to see that, taken in, pardonably enough, by appearances, they had ascribed intentions to their former Premier which he had never entertained. They had ascribed racial animosity to one who had been their friend, and whom they knew by experience to have no racial animosity at all.

Mr. Rhodes had simply aimed at enabling the Uitlanders of Johannesburg to overthrow the corrupt and tyrannous autocracy at Pretoria; but he had never aimed at enabling the Englishman to trample upon the national feeling and the freedom of the Boer. The Transvaal, under President Kruger's increasingly unjust and oppressive legislation, designed to set race against race, had become a menace to the peace of South Africa. The affair of the Drifts in the autumn of 1895 had almost brought the Cape Colony and England into conflict with the Transvaal, entirely through President Kruger's attempt to squeeze the Cape Dutchman into submission, by quadrupling the charge made for entry into the Johannesburg market. The Transvaal Government, too, was the one obstacle to the Union of South Africa, the union that is of commercial interests, of customs, and railways. This union the Cape Colonist had learned from Mr. Rhodes to desire. President Kruger alone barred the way.

Then again, President Kruger's Government, with its hostility to British ideas and interests, and its encouragement of Hollander and German, was a magnet to attract the interference of the only foreign power that had definite ambitions in South Africa. It was against the Hollander and the German element, and against the tyranny of the Kruger clique, that Mr. Rhodes aided the Uitlanders to strike, and the Cape Dutchman, a very reasonable personage, when not carried away by his feelings, has had time for reflection and has perceived the truth.

It is to the credit of his intelligence that he has perceived this for himself; for President Kruger, through his emissaries, and Mr. Hofmeyr, through his caucus, have done their best to obscure the true issue. President Kruger may, it is possible, really imagine that Mr. Rhodes intended to seize the Rand to fill the coffers of the Chartered Company, though it is difficult to understand how so shrewd and experienced a man of affairs could seriously entertain a proposition so manifestly absurd; but Mr. Hofmeyr, a man of well-balanced mind as well as great ability, surely knows better. Mr. Rhodes's plan of aiding Johannesburg to obtain its political rights, and referring the question of the flag to the sovereign will of the whole people of the South African Republic was, if the Cape Dutchman considers it dispassionately, far less open to criticism from the **Dutch** standpoint, than the arrangement by which the Cape Colony was to pay **half the** expense of an Imperial force sent up to enforce Mr. Chamberlain's ultimatum about the closing of the Drifts in the autumn of 1895. Yet the Cape Dutchman, through the Cape Ministry, consented very reasonably to this arrangement; because his material interests were seriously injured and his anger aroused **by President** Kruger's despotic and hostile action.

Of course, the irregularity of the means employed in Mr. Rhodes's plan to make the Transvaal a free republic in **fact** as well as in name cannot be denied; **but** only a red-tape righteousness would take that irregularity very seriously. The Cape Dutchman has **now had** time to reflect; he sees the truth; and highly **to** his own credit has received back with **open arms his old** chief, " the Englishman with the Afrikander heart," who by his freedom from racial feeling, and by his fidelity to local **self-**

government, has reconciled our Dutch fellow-subjects to the British Empire.

Treat the South African Dutchman with consideration, fairness, and justice, and there is no better citizen to be found. Downing Street has treated him very badly in the past, and the English press is even now too much in the habit of depreciating the good qualities, and exaggerating the deficiencies of the Boer. Those Englishmen who knew them well gave a very different report. Ask Mr. Selous what he thinks of his old friend the distinguished sportsman, Cornelius Van Rooyen, or Mr. Millais what he thinks of the admirable Roelof Van Staden, the very *beau-ideal* of a hunter and a man, or turn to the candid pages of one, whose *forte* is fault-finding, I mean Major A. G. Leonard, and observe his admissions as to the former of these two admirable specimens of the Boer.

It was not against the South African Dutchman individually; but against the tyranny of the German and Hollander clique at Pretoria, headed by President **Kruger**, that Mr. Rhodes's policy has been **directed**; for that policy with its aim of a United South Africa under England's hegemony, with free institutions, equal justice, and common commercial interests, is **as** much for the benefit of the South African Dutch**man as of the** Afrikander of English race and speech. **That in the** application of his policy **the** great Statesman stumbled for once, in **a** rough-and-ready attempt **to** hastily remove **an** obstacle, is a mistake, **the** Cape Dutchman perceives, that merely requires to be treated with the forbearance and common sense which must be exercised, since **to err is** human, towards every statesman **at** some point in his career. **When he puts the** single error beside the immense and far-reaching benefits **attained, and still** attainable, for **South** Africans by **the policy and the** statesmanship of Mr. Rhodes, the error becomes microscopic, and may be **treated as** invisible.

The Cape Dutchman, then, has shrewdly discovered for himself the true inwardness of the situation. He sees that Jameson's inroad to aid the rising at Johannesburg is merely a single mistake in the game which Mr. Rhodes, as the representative of South African progress and South African Union, resulting in the peaceful fusion of races into a United South African people, has been playing for years, and is still playing, with President Kruger as the representative of a retrogressive ideal, a positively mediæval despotism; a despotism with a policy of jealous isolation, backed by foreign support, which, were it successful, must result, not in an ultimate Dutch ascendency, but in the substitution for the freedom-bringing British hegemony of the cast-iron Officialism of Germany.

No one would suffer more than the freedom-loving South African Dutchman if England were to lose to Germany her headship in South Africa; and this the more intelligent

Cape Colony Dutchman has already perceived for himself. That he should not have perceived it in the first blaze of indignation in January, 1895, is only natural; and it would be well if all Englishmen were as free from that fault-finding self-righteousness which is near of kin to hypocrisy, as those Dutchmen of the Western Province, who have welcomed back Mr. Rhodes, and acclaimed his return to political life with undiminished confidence in the general trend of his policy of progress, in spite of the admitted error of judgment in his connection with the Transvaal revolutionary movement.

And here it may be well to observe that, though the return to Mr. Rhodes of the confidence of the Dutch electorate in Cape Colony was, until his recent triumphal progress, uncertain, many of the Dutch members of the Afrikander Bond and of the Assembly spoke out boldly long ago with a good sense and a statesmanlike breadth of view, which may be pondered with advantage by Mr. Rhodes's own countrymen here in England. As long ago as last March Mr. Bellingan, a member of the Upper Chamber at Cape Town, and of the Bond, spoke of the great services which Mr. Rhodes had rendered to the Colony, and refused to have anything to do with the outcry against him. Even if the worst were proved, that Mr. Rhodes sent Dr. Jameson into the Transvaal, one mistake could not (he said) undo all his previous great services to South Africa. Observe that this large-minded Dutch member of the Afrikander Bond calls Mr. Rhodes's conduct, taking it at its worst, a " mistake "—and, in truth, that is exactly what it is—a mistake in the means employed to achieve a most praiseworthy purpose.

CHAPTER XIII.

THE JUDGMENT OF ENGLAND.

It might have been supposed that the verdict of his own countrymen upon Mr. Rhodes, upon the single ill-judged, yet, all things considered, not unpardonable act in a public career of unrivalled usefulness and extraordinary distinction, would have been well-nigh unanimous. Apparently, the attitude of a small section of politicians, Little Englanders themselves, or eager to make capital for party purposes, and of a small section of the press, keen to discover the flaws in a great man, or willing to be made the tools of private animosity, leaves English opinion on Mr. Rhodes divided.

To this must be added the disposition of a

considerable number of Englishmen to-day to judge public actions by a standard, I will not say of unctuous, but rather of red-tape, righteousness. Yet there are precedents in our own time which justify a very generous attitude towards the irregular action of Mr. Rhodes. Garibaldi organized in a friendly state his expedition to overthrow the Bourbon tyranny in Sicily. Cavour connived at Garibaldi's action. The Powers of Europe broke out in a storm of indignation against this " act of piracy against a friendly state," and yet because the Sicilians had real and deep grievances, England approved of Garibaldi's action. Nor was it only the great body of the nation who applauded the Italian patriot's highly irregular action. Lord John Russell, our responsible Foreign Minister, from the first openly encouraged Garibaldi's enterprise, gave him all the aid in his power, secured the neutrality of France, and permitted our fleet in the Mediterranean to actively express their

English sympathy with a bold stroke for freedom.

Lord John Russell considered Garibaldi's raid "an act of justice and generosity," and approved of Cavour's connivance. His attitude expressed the general attitude of England, and it is a little difficult to see why it should be praiseworthy for an Italian Statesman to encourage a breach of the peace in order to free Italians in a friendly State from an oppressive Government, and blameworthy for an English Statesman to endeavour, in much the same way, to help Englishmen to free themselves from a similar condition of servitude. The fact that the oppressive Government was not English, but a combination of German, Hollander, and Dutch, and the oppressed people, mostly English, surely does not make the case worse against the English Statesman.

It is not, indeed, necessary to go back to Cavour and Garibaldi and the struggle for Italian unification, which is in many ways a parallel to the struggle for South African unification, in the course of which Mr. Rhodes was brought into collision with the opposing forces of German and Hollander intrigue in the Transvaal. The attitude to-day of a large section of English lovers of freedom towards the insurgents in Crete and their Greek supporters, is what one would expect from the nation that applauded Garibaldi.

English sympathisers with Cretan insurgents and Greek raiders are openly working an agitation to aid the insurrection. The King of Greece has gone a great deal further than Mr. Rhodes in sending a force into the territory of a friendly power, without any declaration of war. Prince George of Greece might-give lessons in daring irregularity to Dr. Jameson.

Turkey is a friendly power, and yet we in England cordially approve, and in my opinion are right in approving, of all this highly irregular, and, technically speaking, unjustifiable action. The Lord Chief Justice himself, who has laid it down that "an offence," under the Foreign Enlistment Act, "is complete with the preparing and assisting in the preparation or aiding and abetting in the preparation," of an expedition against a friendly State, has nothing to say against the collection of funds to aid and abet the Cretan insurrection; nor are the Members of Parliament, who urge on the Greek raiders and hold public meetings to support them; nor papers like the *Daily Chronicle*, which wax ecstatic in praise of Colonel Vassos and his bold filibusters, in the least restrained by the heavy sentence passed last year on Englishmen, who, in order to assist their oppressed fellow-countrymen, committed a similar breach of the law. With reason may Mr. Rhodes and all South African Imperialists who backed him in his irregular action, rub their eyes and ask if they are dreaming.

Is this the England that was so shocked at help given to the Transvaal Reformers? Is this the same England that last year helped President Kruger to disarm Johannesburg, and now allows Greek transports to land their raiders in Turkish territory, although the Turkish Government has left the whole business of checking Greece in the hands of England and the other Powers.

The reason for the inconsistency is this— England does not believe in the reality of grievances of British subjects in the Transvaal, while believing implicitly in the grievances of Turkish subjects in Crete. Sir William Harcourt calls the Uitlander movement Mr. Rhodes's revolution, and he merely expresses what many still believe—that there were no real grievances, and no general discontent.

Well might Cape Afrikanders and Transvaal reformers despair of a government which, by its apathy, forced the oppressed Englishmen of the Transvaal to help themselves, and ask the help of Mr. Rhodes, and which, when it did intervene, intervened with cynical success, only to rivet the chains more firmly than ever on the oppressed **community** in Johannesburg. If only they had been Cretans or Italians or Greeks, the Uitlanders would have had the sympathy and support their condition required; but being **of** English race, they have apparently little to expect but misrepresentation of their motives, and self-righteous condemnation of the slightest irregularity.

Mr. Chamberlain, **indeed, has somewhat** tardily shown that he has too much real statesmanship to ignore the fact that any inquiry into the preparations for Jameson's inroad must reach back to the causes of that inroad. The immediate cause, **of** course, was the long-smouldering discontent at Johannesburg. **It** was not Mr. Rhodes who kindled that **discon-**tent. It was not the Reform leaders. Behind Mr. Rhodes, behind the Reform leaders, is **to** be found the undoubted first cause of the discontent at Johannesburg, **of** the projected insurrection, of the assistance of Mr. Rhodes, of the ill-starred inroad of Dr. Jameson, and that formidable first cause of the whole Transvaal trouble is none other than the old Dopper Dictator himself. Just as the misgovernment of the Sultan is the guilty first cause of the insurrection in Crete, so the misgovernment of the Transvaal President was the guilty first cause of the trouble on the Rand, which, in its turn, produced the Raid.

No jury of intelligent and impartial men, who had fully examined into the whole problem, could come to any other conclusion than that it is the policy of President Kruger and the spirit in which it has been pursued, which has produced the action of the Johannesburg Reformers, the action of Mr. Rhodes, the action of Dr. Jameson.

With rare generosity, England conceded to the Boers the independence they claimed, and conceded it when defeat had made concession require considerable self-abnegation.

The status of citizens and the rights of citizenship were virtually guaranteed to Englishmen in the Transvaal by the Convention which confirmed the retrocession. English enterprise and capital, after years of persevering labour, solved the problem of the Rand, the proper treatment of refractory pyritic ores, and demonstrated the value of the gold-mines, which achievements have raised the income of the Republic from eighty thousand to over four millions. Englishmen fashioned the key of the storehouse of material prosperity, and placed it in the hands of the unenterprising Boer. The reward of making the Transvaal the richest state in South Africa has been that, in the Transvaal alone in Africa, Englishmen are oppressed and treated with contempt, and England is regarded as the enemy, the influence of whose free institutions and free commerce must be kept at arms' length by a policy of jealous exclusion and isolation. While Mr. Rhodes, at the Cape, was bringing

Boer and Englishman together, melting away the old rivalries of race by a policy of consideration and conciliation, President Kruger, in the Transvaal, was doing his utmost to stir bad blood between the races, and to prove his love of peace by legislation of unconcealed hostility to Englishmen and English interests.

At first the Englishmen of the Randt were strongly in favour of President Kruger, they supported his election, and were thoroughly loyal to his Government. By a deliberate and persistent course of injury and insult he has completely alienated them. By a succession of promises, occasionally kept to the eye, but invariably broken as to the fulfilment, he has sapped their faith in his word and their confidence in his good intentions. While he was dangling before them the hope of citizenship, he has laboured only too successfully to place the reality of citizenship completely out of their reach. With deliberate intention he has raised to such a price by his exorbitant tariffs the simplest necessaries of life—such as flour and bacon, that the English workman or artizan cannot afford to maintain a household, and must not marry, or, if married, must leave his wife and children behind him in England, and thus become a temporary sojourner in a land in which he would like to establish himself as a permanent citizen.

A long course of injury and injustice which had made the native-born subjects of Queen Victoria the unenfranchised serfs of the Transvaal Dopper, succeeded in stirring up widespread discontent in Johannesburg, which, after smouldering for years, broke out in a constitutional agitation in 1892, and, beaten back contemptuously by the President and the ruling clique at Pretoria, flamed up at last in 1895 in the revolutionary movement at Johannesburg, of which the raid was a mere subsidiary incident.

The discontent at Johannesburg was not the work of Mr. Rhodes; that discontent came from the intolerable tyranny of President Kruger, which had gone on piling up injustices and creating grievances, till the load was more than free-born Englishmen or Cape Colonists could bear.   President Kruger, with his German and Hollander officials, is responsible for the grievances which alone caused, and which fully justified, the revolutionary movement to obtain relief; he is responsible for the revolutionary movement, caused by his deliberate policy, and, therefore, he is also the responsible and guilty first cause of the Jameson raid, which was simply an error in the use of one of the instruments of the revolutionary programme.

It cannot be doubted that the verdict of all reasonable Englishmen, when they are acquainted with the whole truth, will be that the grievances of the Uitlanders were ample justification for the revolution, even had it fully come to maturity; and as for the raid (apart, of course, from the question of its being ill-timed), their verdict will take account of Lord John Russell's attitude to the very similar enterprize of Garibaldi, and say with Lord John Russell's avowed guide, Vattel, " When a people, from good reasons, take up arms against an oppressor, it is but an act of justice and generosity to assist," as Prince George of Greece has been assisting the Cretan insurgents, as Jameson attempted to assist the Reformers of Johannesburg.

Those who desire to arrive at a just conclusion upon Mr. Rhodes's connection with the events which have been made the subject of the Inquiry by the Parliamentary Committee, should be careful to remember the words of one of the wisest and most experienced of our representatives in South Africa, who, like Mr. Rhodes, advocated and suffered for his advocacy of a policy of South African Federation, I mean Sir George Grey : " Can a man, who, on a distant and exposed frontier, surrounded by difficulties, . . . assumes a responsibility, guided by many circumstances which he can neither record nor remember, as they come hurrying on, one after the other, be fairly judged of in respect to the amount of responsibility he assumes, by those who, in the quiet of distant offices in London, know nothing of the anxieties or of the nature of the difficulties he had to encounter."

A great deal of latitude must be permitted to a statesman who, like Mr. Rhodes, had to maintain the very existence of the British hegemony against the encroachments of President Kruger, with his scheme of an exclusively Dutch supremacy. That this has long been President Kruger's cherished scheme I have pointed out, and recent evidence corroborates this view. President Kruger has formed a close alliance with his kinsmen of the Free State, and armament has been obtained for both Republics regardless of expense. Nor is President Kruger without allies at the Cape, so long as Mr. Hofmeyr dominates the Bond, or allies in

London, to whom the latest reinforcement is
Mr. J. W. Sauer. From a well-informed Cape
source the following highly instructive story is
derived; the story is, I believe, authentic. A
Dutch leader, who is a very resourceful individual, was the original narrator.

"I don't know," said he, " if you know how
two of us stopped the Imperial troops from
going up through Cape Colony to deal with
the Transvaal Rebellion in 1880-1 ? We got
up a rifle range at Rondebosch and offered
prizes for shooting, and forty or fifty Dutchmen used to come and practise there. We
let the news leak out to the Governor that the
Cape Dutchmen were practising rifle-shooting
and preparing to resist the Imperial troops. The
Governor sent home the news that we were
practising at the rifle ranges with the Dutchmen, and it would be very dangerous to bring
the Imperial troops up to the Transvaal by way
of Cape Town." The result was they were sent
round by Natal, and forced to advance through

the Drakenberg Range, where the Boers had very strong positions and absolutely safe cover. The repulse of Laing's Nek, and the disaster at Majuba Hill were the consequences of this little game of Dutch "Bluff."

How the Dutch leader must smile while he watches Mr. J. W. Sauer playing to-day the very same game here in London. Mr. Sauer has been spending his time over here in preaching the anti-British Dutchmen's doctrine of 1880-1, that, if there was to be war between England and the Transvaal, the whole Cape Colony Dutchmen would rise in support of the Transvaal. Mr. Chamberlain, it is to be supposed, has too much good sense and too much strength to be imposed upon by the "bluff" that was so successful on a weak Colonial Secretary in 1880-81; but it will do him no harm to understand the purposes and the value of Mr. Sauer's alarmist views.

And just as immediately before the insurrection and the retrocession of the Transvaal,

Messrs. Kruger and Joubert had been actively canvassing in the Dutch districts of the Cape Colony; so now we find Sir James Sivewright, in his speech at Worcester, in the Dutch district, obliged to protest against similar tactics, boldly giving his reasons to the special correspondent, at Cape Town, of the *Standard and Diggers' News:* "Am I to stand quietly by while some, under guise of demanding punishment and redress for the raid, are looking far beyond, and taking occasion by the hand, are aiming at the establishment of a South African Republic from the Cape to the Zambesi?"

The Republic which Sir James Sivewright, himself a member of the Afrikander Bond, refers to, would be Dutch-German not British. What a combination of the unctuous autocracy of Pretoria with the meddling officialism of Berlin would make such a nominal republic to be, it is not difficult to imagine, though it is certain that German officialism would have to find its victims among the Uitlanders, for the Boer is a staunch Individualist, whose views would delight the heart of Mr. Auberon Hubert. An inconsiderable fraction of the official interference, to which the Uitlanders are obliged to submit in the Transvaal, would have long ago raised every Boer in South Africa in rebellion—an attitude highly creditable to the Dutchman's love of freedom, which would however be more admirable if he saw the justice of treating others as he insists on being treated himself.

Not unnaturally the Transvaal Boer, unable to understand the trustful reliance of loyal British subjects on the British Government, looks upon the patient endurance of the Uitlanders as due to lack of self-reliance and manhood, and despises them accordingly. Thus the shame of English residents in the retrocession of the Transvaal by Mr. Gladstone, is renewed in an acuter form to-day in the apparent desertion of the Uitlanders by their

Mother Country, in a land where **that Mother Country** is the Suzerain Power.

"**No** local causes," **says** President Kruger, severely criticizing Mr. Chamberlain's statesmanlike speech on the motion to abandon the Committee **of** Inquiry, "existed to justify such a criminal raid," and added, "I have always used, **and am** still using, **my** influence to diminish **race** hatred **in South Africa.**" To point to the condition of the Transvaal, where President Kruger has ruled for many years autocratically, and where race rivalry and race animosity, stimulated by all the efforts of legislation, have reached their acutest development, is the best answer to this statement. President Kruger, when he came into office, found the Uitlanders well disposed and friendly ; he **has** made them, by a succession of deliberately hostile measures, what they now are. He **has had** a free hand in the Transvaal, **and the** condition of the majority of his population **is** his own deliberate **work.**

Since Mr. Rhodes's resignation and temporary retirement President Kruger has been the solitary great personage in South Africa, and this briefly is his record. Before Johannesburg had disarmed and resigned the idea of striking a blow for its liberties, he promised reform, and assured the Uitlanders that he was ready to forget and forgive. Since then he has shown his forgiveness by sentences of imprisonment and heavy fines, and his forgetfulness of the past by legislation that would have been considered scandalous had it issued from the Yildiz Kiosk. It would be enough to instance two laws only; the law to give the President power to expel any alien without right of appeal to the courts, and the law by which he is enabled to suppress any newspaper which displeases him—the New Press Law and the Aliens Expulsion Law, of which the former has been brought to bear actively on the admirable and independent *Critic*, the property of Mr. Hess.

It must be observed that the mere fact that these laws exist, even without any actual enforcement, establishes a reign of terror, and takes away the freedom, and influences the action of every British subject in the Transvaal.

To these two laws he has added the insolent Aliens Admission law ; in which the new passport system has been contrived for the purpose, which it has very successfully accomplished, of destroying the status of Englishmen and Cape Colonists in South Africa. A pass had previously been required only from natives, and now respectable citizens (witness the recent insulting conduct of the police to Mr. John Morrogh, lately member of the British House of Commons, in the streets of Johannesburg), because they are British subjects, are degraded in the eyes of the native population to the level of Kaffirs. The effects of this degradation will be far-reaching, and are already being felt in native disturbances in various parts of the Cape Colony.

Born in the Cape Colony, but a voluntary exile, when a mere child, owing to his parents' objection to the suppression of slavery by the British Government, President Kruger's antipathy to the British Government is what Hannibal's probably was to the Roman Republic. It is against the success of this monstrous anti-British policy of Pretoria that Mr. Cecil Rhodes has striven ever since he put a stop to President Kruger's filibustering republics in Bechuanaland, in 1884, and headed him back in his attempt, under the baffled claim-jumper, Colonel Ferreira, to "jump" the Northern territory in 1891.

The proper way of regarding the so-called Jameson raid, which was a mere incident of the Revolutionary Movement at Johannesburg (even if that raid had been directly Mr. Rhodes's doing), is as a single ineffectual blow dealt in the interests of British hegemony, somewhat in the fashion of many dealt by

President Kruger in the development of his anti-British policy.

The British Government has neither asked nor received compensation for the succession of raids accomplished or attempted by President Kruger's people. It has taken a common-sense view of them, and has considered that in the frontier policy of a new country like South Africa, great latitude must be allowed to irregular and, strictly speaking, unconstitutional methods which could not be allowed (except in the case of Cretans, Greeks or Italians) in Europe. This latitude has been continually allowed to the anti-British policy of President Kruger. Is it solely denied to the pro-British policy of Mr. Rhodes? Even the Vienna and Paris press are able to perceive the reasonableness of this requirement, and see in Mr. Rhodes "a maker of States, a pioneer of civilisation, a figure of almost superhuman power. Such a man must not be judged in a narrow-minded spirit."

At the Inquiry Mr. Rhodes has been frankness itself; he has not attempted to conceal anything that concerns his own personal part in the Transvaal trouble. He has taken on himself the whole blame of the admittedly unconstitutional action. His obvious ignorance of the ill-judged telegrams, and other proceedings of well-meaning but hasty subordinates, should be borne in mind by those who attempt to judge his action, by the English people as well as by the Select Committee. In his loyalty to timid representatives he has generously accepted the entire responsibility for blunders with which he had personally nothing to do. All this must be taken into account if England is to avoid grave injustice to the statesman and the man.

Finally, the English people will do well to remember the words of Burke, when on his defence before the electors of Bristol, words which apply admirably to the Inquiry that is going on at Westminster :—" Most certainly it is our duty to examine; it is our interest, too. But it must be with discretion. With an attention to all the circumstances and all the motives, like sound judges and not like cavilling pettifoggers and quibbling pleaders, prying into flaws and hunting for exceptions. Look, gentlemen, to the whole tenor of your member's conduct. . . . He may have fallen into errors, he must have faults; but our error is greater and our fault is radically ruinous to ourselves if we do not bear, if we do not even applaud, the whole compound and mixed mass of such a character."

CHAPTER XIV.

AN APPRECIATION OF A GREAT STATESMAN.

To know the life-work of Cecil Rhodes, which
I have endeavoured to unfold in the preceding
chapters, is to know, to a great extent, the
man; and to glance at the map of South
Africa is to measure his stature in his public
life. His portrait in words may serve, however, to enable the reader to understand more
clearly what manner of man he is. The
first impression he makes is somewhat dis-
appointing. One expects so much; one's imagination is fired by his achievements; and
one sees so little of what one expects. A
big, heavily-built, indolent-looking man, some
six feet in height, carelessly dressed, is what

meets the eye. You might almost take him for a typical English country gentleman, whose talk was of bullocks and turnips, when he was not fox-hunting or shooting. The strong, solid-looking, sunburnt and ruddy face, with the dreamy grey eyes, that seem to gaze into vacancy, shows, when at rest, little sign of extraordinary energy or resolution. Still, if you are a physiognomist, the large intellectual head, the strong chin and firm mouth, cannot fail to convey an impression of strength. Besides, the face which is changed since first I knew it years ago, bears now the deeply marked lines of arduous life, of the life of one who has greatly dared and greatly suffered, who, undeterred by any difficulties, still sets himself to accomplish the great work he was born to do. The side-face, if you watch it at rest, is still more remarkable. It struck me, the first time I saw it years ago, as having the massive strength, impervious to ordinary emotions, of some old Roman emperor, born to command the nations, and care-less of the opinion, whether praise or blame, of the world of lesser men he dominated.

As you get to know him, you gradually receive an impression of impenetrable depth, of an inner being, impossible to read com-pletely, which adds the interest of the unknown to his personality. A physical restlessness, springing from inexhaustible nervous energy, finds expression in perfectly unconscious movements, and occasionally makes him rise from his seat and stride up and down the room. This gives the suggestion of a big reserve force latent behind the impassive ex-terior. Such is the impression he makes, until some thought, or something that is said, pene-trates below the surface and reveals the real man, and then the dreamy grey eyes flash blue, the impassive face lights up, the head bends for-ward decisively, and the strong-willed, large-brained leader of men stands confessed. When he is thus aroused, the indolent look is gone in

an instant, and the words that before had
been listless are succeeded by words that leap
straight to the heart of the subject. One knows
that one is in the presence of a great man—
a big elemental force not easy to measure or
define. This sense of unmeasured largeness of
brain and extraordinary will-power flashes on
one, of course, only occasionally. In his general
conversation, Mr. Rhodes, without being a
brilliant, can be, when he chooses, a fascinating
talker, because he is a perfectly independent
thinker, who speaks straight out what is
uppermost in his mind. He has studied the
world of men much more than the world of
books, though even in the world of books
his reading is considerable and his criticism
independent and stimulating. As a talker he
is entirely unaffected and free from self-
consciousness, and in talk, as in manners, a
hater of conventionality. He does not attempt
to conceal his feelings, when irritated; and
if his genial mood charms, his brusqueness

verges on rudeness. He bluntly calls things by their proper names, and gives his opinion frankly without any view to the effect on his hearers. Thus he pointed out, to the horror of Mr. Gladstone, that his Home Rule Bill merely created a taxed republic, and would be followed by an agitation for representation or separation. A certain large carelessness of appearances distinguishes everything about him, even to his dress and his gestures. His sound sense and outlook on life as it is, would have delighted Carlyle, and made him rank Rhodes among his kingly men, in the same class as Cromwell. His talk is interesting, because one feels it is the expression of a man of deeds, not of a spinner of language. Essentially a man of ideas, his ideas find their natural embodiment in action. Not in speaking or writing, but in doing, not in words but in deeds, he finds the proper expression for his powerful personality.

He is ambitious, but his vast ambitions lift

him far above the petty egotisms that are the vice of the lesser ambitions. His ambition is to do the work for which Nature has fitted him, to be the instrument of British expansion, to be the builder of British Empire, the extender of British ideas and institutions; and he has no more doubt that this is his appointed work in life than he has that, however strong opposing circumstances and forces may seem to be, he will inevitably accomplish the work appointed.

He knows what he has got to do in life, and he means and expects to do it. The consequence is that the misfortunes of last year, which would have wrecked or seriously shattered a lesser man, have made wonderfully little impression on him.

Of course he can adapt himself to circumstances, and can be when he chooses a diplomatist with diplomatists; but naturally, he is frankness itself, and he seldom goes against his nature. Being in reality modest, and

even shy, he dislikes publicity, and would ask
nothing better than to be let alone. With
the abuse of the press he occasionally amuses
himself; but the praise he carefully avoids.
He blushes to be discovered doing good, and
accident alone reveals occasionally some portion of his hidden charities. He regards with
contempt the attitude of London Society,
which courts him again, when it sees his star
is in the ascendant.

The conventions of society merely bore him.
He cares for realities alone. A man with him
is judged simply for what is in him, and
judged with a penetrating insight that very
seldom errs. Set Mr. Rhodes in a roomful of
magnates, and you will probably find he has
picked out some unknown person to talk
to, if, perchance, that unknown person has
brains.

He impresses one in all he does, in his talk,
as in his deeds, as a believer in reality and a
contemner of appearances. The downright

bluff, English sincerity of the man slips out
in his speeches as well as in his conversation,
and sometimes makes his utterances inju-
dicious, witness the "unctuous rectitude"
descriptive of Lord Russell. Perhaps the
basis of the unquestionable charm which Mr.
Rhodes possesses for men of many minds is
this sterling reality, which is frankly without
conventional veneer itself, and is a magnet to
reality in others. He cares not for names,
but things. Provided that he wields the real
power, someone else may have the official
title. He would make the poorest of con-
spirators, for to simulate what is not, or to dis-
simulate what is, is against the law of his
nature. The same belief in reality has shown
itself in his sure and steady methods of company management and finance—methods which
pay attention only to actual results, look to the
slow effect of these results in the future, and
despise the specious unreality of the financial
puff and the "boom."

He cares nothing for any kind of display, and only the stress of circumstances led him to the decisive action by which he proved the greatness of his manhood, when, with cool courage and absolute self-reliance, he went up to the Matopos, confident that he could overcome, by his unaided influence, the rebel Matabele, at bay in their rocky fastnesses.

It was the solid reality of the work to be done, which was nothing less than the preservation of Rhodesia, that induced him to take the risk, and, as a result, he discovered himself to the eyes of an astonished world, a millionaire and financier, who was also at heart one of the heroes. In a time when money is the great power, the value of this example of high-tempered courage, in a class not famous for courage, is difficult to over-estimate.

Being a man of ideas, a great practical genius in his own way, he is, as might be expected, what is called eccentric. That is to say, he is out of the common in everything.

He hates writing even the shortest letter, and prepares his speeches, down to the most complicated statistics, solely in his own head. The convention of answering a letter used certainly not to appeal to him some years ago, when I have often seen him stuff a voluminous correspondence into a drawer, with the observation, "Most of them will answer themselves." His immense capacity for work is aided by his regular habits of life. In Africa at six o'clock every morning he is in the saddle, for a spell of hard riding exercise, being unable to get a free hour during his working day. Hard work and absorption in his big schemes keep him unmarried. He makes this sacrifice, as he makes many others, to the ideal of the British Empire, to which his life is devoted.

Of his unconventionality there are endless anecdotes, from the refusal of admission to him at the Kimberley Exhibition, the result of his habit of wearing an old suit and a hat that may once have been new, and carrying no purse and no money to pay for entrance, to the story of his non-appearance at the opening of a function, at which he had to preside near Cape Town, when the missing Premier, after an anxious search, was discovered disporting himself, in happy forgetfulness, in the bay, his clothes piled up just beyond the reach of the water.

Any estimate of Mr. Rhodes would be incomplete which did not note the absence of all love of money for itself, a remarkable thing in a millionaire, who has made his own millions by years of intense application and the exercise of inexhaustible energy. He has none of the expensive tastes or the love of luxury or ostentation that belong to the ordinary millionaire. No man has lived and lives more simply. For years after he was the head of the De Beers Mines, and many times a millionaire, he lived at Kimberley in modest rooms and took his meals at the club, spending no more on himself than an ordinary man would have done who had less than one-hundredth part of his income. At the same time he thought nothing of giving £10,000 to Mr. Parnell, on definite terms which bound him to a clause in the Home Rule Bill for permissive representation of the Colonies at Westminster; of course, with a view to aid Colonial Federation. Nor did he hesitate to supply eight times the amount to equip Jameson's expedition for the first Matabele War, or a yet larger sum to carry the pioneer of civilization, the Trans-Continental Telegraph, across Africa.

Four-fifths of the capital to extend the telegraph from Table Bay to Tanganyika has been supplied by Mr. Rhodes, because the public, seeing no prospect of dividends in the near future, naturally would not subscribe. The only profit immediately available was the benefit to British civilisation, the aid to British expansion, which this means of swift communication would bring. With this sort of dividend there is nobody except Mr. Rhodes that will be satisfied—of course, a proof, as Mr. Labouchere would tell us, of his greed.

The idea was Mr. Rhodes's own, and in spite of the warnings of practical men, who pointed out that the natives over hundreds of miles of savage country, would cut and steal the wires, iron wire being a possession they prize highly, he carried out his idea. He had made a fortune to use in the cause of Empire and civilization, and he did not hesitate to use it. As he said once to General Gordon, in his homely way, "It is no use our having mazy ideas; it is no use giving vent to our imaginations. If we have imaginative ideas we must have pounds, shillings, and pence to carry them out."

Again, just as he carried the telegraph line across Africa at his own expense, so he was obliged to supply the whole of the money to build the extension of the Beira Railway, in order to give a communication to Eastern Rhodesia. In short, everywhere it will be found

Mr. Rhodes has used his wealth freely with a high purpose for the expansion of the Empire and the advantage of the English race.

Mr. Rhodes has been sometimes called cynical. He is no cynic at heart, but he dislikes—and does not hesitate to show his dislike to—meanness in others, naturally expecting that his own large generosity should provoke some response. He subscribed, as I have just pointed out, the bulk of the capital of the Trans-Continental Telegraph Company, but expected some patriotic support. He got none; except, indeed, ten pounds from that widely-regretted officer, best of sportsmen and good fellows, Major Roddy Owen. The British public will put their money into a telegraph company only if certain of good interest. They like patriotism as they like philanthropy, with five per cent. on their investment. Mr. Rhodes met with a poor response to his appeal to the companies he has done most for. The De Beers shareholders sent nothing, apart from Mr. Rhodes's personal friends. The Gold-fields of South Africa shareholders sent nothing, with the exception of one angry shareholder, who wrote to know who paid for the stamps and paper of the appeal. After all he had done for the shareholders of De Beers and Gold-fields, Mr. Rhodes thought they might have assisted him; and disgusted at their attitude, observed to a friend, with a touch of not unnatural cynicism, that he was not surprised shareholders were robbed.

Nor has, apparently, the British Government learned from the generosity of Mr. Rhodes to all Imperial objects to act with common justice, I will not say equal generosity, when they have business dealings with him. When the Chartered Company came to settle its accounts in Nyasaland and the North with the British Government, on the Government taking over the Nyasaland Protectorate, this was their idea of fair play. The large subsidy of the Chartered Company for the Northern territory, which was now to be divided, the Company taking the administration of their own part, had been spent entirely in the territory which the Government took over. The Government had the whole benefit of the expenditure, but refused to repay the Company, though not a shilling had been spent in the Company's territory. Worse than this : A distinguished Imperial officer, Captain Maguire, had been killed in battle with a slave-raiding chief, and his head stuck up as a trophy over the Slaver's kraal-gate. This happened in the territory of the Imperial Protectorate where the slave-raiding chief was the terror of the country. Mr. Rhodes gave £10,000 out of his own pocket to break up the slaver's power, and an expedition, under Sir Harry Johnston, effected the desired object. The expedition in which Captain Maguire was killed was an Imperial expedition, the slaver chief was in Imperial territory, yet when the account came to be settled, the Government refused to pay Mr.

Rhodes on the grounds that **the** expedition made, and the expense incurred, had not been authorised by the Imperial authorities.

A great part of Mr. Rhodes's life has been spent in hard work, chiefly in the diamond **fields.** To see him engaged in this work of the diamond mines, the work of money-making, is to see the man in his real character, under the least advantageous circumstances. For this reason **I** will venture to turn to Kimberley nearly ten years ago, and show Mr. Rhodes at work.

It was the evening of a day nearly ten years **ago,** when three men, who held the chief interest in the diamond mines at Kimberley, sat down together to arrange the terms **of the** projected amalgamation. The three were Mr. Cecil Rhodes, **Mr.** Alfred Beit, and Mr. B. J. Barnato of the Kimberley Mine. Each one had a concession he required from the others, but the requirements of the first two are of no public interest. The concession Mr. Rhodes required was entirely different. It was this: " I want the power to go to the North to carry out the expansion there, and I think the Company might assist me in the work. I believe everything they give will be returned; but even if it were lost, it is a very fair case for the doctrine of ransom." In other words, Mr. Rhodes insisted on getting the power to use the profits of the De Beers Mine for the acquisition of the unoccupied regions to the North. Mr. Beit said little, but supported Mr. Rhodes; but the notion of using the diamond mines to create an Empire did not recommend itself as good business to Mr. Barnato, even when it was backed by Mr. Rhodes. Mr. Barnato was amused at this proposal, and argued against it for a long time. But Mr. Rhodes was determined to have his way, and insisted on their agreeing to his condition, as he had agreed to theirs. He sat there with them all night, and till four o'clock in the morning. At last the other two gave way, Mr. Barnato observing,

"Some people have a fancy for this thing, some for that thing, but you have a fancy for making an Empire. Well, I suppose we must give it you."

Thus Cecil Rhodes got the trust deed of the De Beers Company changed, and so De Beers furnished £500,000 to carry out the work of establishing our Empire in the North, and the fact that we possess Rhodesia is due largely to his action upon that memorable evening.

This use of the De Beers money is characteristic of Mr. Rhodes, who considers that millionaire companies, as well as individual millionaires, ought to be willing to use a portion of their money for the public good, when an opportunity presents itself, and so Mr. Rhodes's millionaire friends have been led by him to take their part, of course in a lesser degree, as promoters of the public good, and set an example of public spirit and sense of responsibility for the use of wealth to millionaires

all the world over. Furthermore, the De
Beers Company itself is an example of the
largeness and liberality of spirit with which
Mr. Rhodes administers even a joint-stock
business.

It is a valuable example of that high con-
science, that sense of responsibility in money-
making and money-spending, which is so rare,
and is at the same time so necessary if the
moralization of capital is ever to be attained.
This, which is one of the pressing problems of
our time, is seen in the De Beers Company to
have at least approached a solution. Whether
it be in the matter of an Exhibition, or a Sani-
tarium, expenses for Schools, or for Rifle Volunteers, Mr. Rhodes has seen to it that De Beers
does its duty to the people at Kimberley and
forwards the progress and prosperity of the
community.

And yet all this expenditure is made with
such excellent business foresight and skill that
De Beers has actually grown richer by its

liberality. For instance, the £500,000 spent in assisting the Chartered Company was only locked up temporarily, and has now been repaid in full. De Beers have even made a profit, and have the right to any diamond mines found in Rhodesia—a possible but, it must be admitted, improbable contingency. The Company has also a third share in the Northern, that is, the Bechuanaland railway, which is already a paying concern, and in addition it owns a large block of land in the Northern territory. The public benefit conferred by helping the Chartered Company over their difficulties was a great one, but the result has been a profit to De Beers. So, too, the assistance given to the building of the Indwe railway has finally resulted in a large saving of money to De Beers by getting them coal from the Indwe coal mine at a much lower price than they paid elsewhere.

Already Mr. Rhodes has begun to suggest to the shareholders the desirability of another benefit to the public, the encouragement of the fruit industry in the Western Province. Many of the fruit-growers are poor, and want scientific knowledge as well as capital. Mr. Rhodes merely made a tentative suggestion as to this at the last meeting. "It is a public act which, I take it, should be borne in mind, and I hope it will be in this, as in some other public acts in the past, that the De Beers shareholders will have the satisfaction of knowing that they have done something for the country, and also had a substantial return."

I have dwelt at some length on the administration of the De Beers Company because there Mr. Rhodes has been practically supreme, and by an examination of his methods one can gain a very valuable insight into his character.

It is sometimes asserted that Mr. Rhodes is utterly unscrupulous. In his dealings with men he likes to call a spade a spade, and that no doubt is shocking to the rectitude that is more sensitive as to appearances than as to realities.

The success of his career in business comes, after his own immense business ability and farsightedness, not from financial cunning, but from the fairness he shows in appraising the interests of others and the absence of greed in estimating his own. His reputed belief that there is no one with whom he cannot do a deal, rightly understood, does him no discredit, for the reason for this belief is his faith that just and considerate treatment of men wins their adherence, and pays in the long run. The result is what might be expected; those who enter on business relations with him are so well satisfied with his treatment of them, that he has now only to father an enterprise to be certain of their loyal support. Lord Rothschild, for instance, when Charters were at their worst (about ten shillings a share), gave Mr. Rhodes £25,000 towards the building of the railway from the East Coast, though, as Mr. Rhodes has told us in one of his speeches, Lord Rothschild did not believe in the enterprise, and thought he was "chucking his money into the sea."

Having been a great financier before he was a Premier, that giving of various rewards for political services rendered, which no one would question as illegitimate in Lord Salisbury or Lord Rosebery, is called bribery and corruption in Mr. Rhodes; while his critics forget that our whole English system of unsalaried Members of Parliament is built upon the knowledge that political services do not go unrewarded, whatever the form of the reward may be.

Certain it is that any one fairly examining his management of De Beers will discover a full recognition of the doctrine of ransom, and a steady attempt on his part for years past towards the moralization of a Joint-Stock Company, which is surely no small task to undertake and effect in the moral sphere.

What Mr. Rhodes has been found to be as

U

the controlling influence in the De Beers Mines he may be expected to be in his management of the Chartered Company in South Africa; and that, as a matter of fact, he has been found to be in Rhodesia, where the admirable business management has been accompanied by a public-spirited encouragement of progress and enterprise of all kinds, even where, as was generally the case, no immediate return could be expected for the money expended.

The tried and proved success of the far-sighted wisdom of Mr. Rhodes's management of De Beers promises well for the future of the Chartered Company.

There was much adverse criticism when he lent half-a-million of De Beers money to the Chartered Company, and many prophecies that it would all be lost; but the event has proved that he was perfectly right and the shareholders of De Beers have forgotten their past grumblings in their present contemplation of the very substantial profits.

Mr. Rhodes sees further than other men, and the principles of his finance are eminently solid and conservative. He prophesied publicly years ago, at the time of the De Beers amalgamation, that the old £5 shares would go to £70. This seemed the wildest optimism at the time. Yet remembering that the old shares had been split, one finds that they work out nearly £60 at present, while they worked out £4 higher last year. Remembering, also, that last year's profit was only £1,900,000, while in the last six months the profits have been £1,200,000, one sees that his prophecy is within measurable distance of realization.

The conservative financial methods of Mr. Rhodes may be further seen in the fact that he has not only bought out of the earnings several mines, such as the Wesselton mine, for £460,000; but has laid by a reserve fund in Consols of one-and-a-quarter millions. Only very gradually has he allowed the dividends to increase. Provision has been made for

almost every possible eventuality. Slow and
sure is his motto in finance. He keeps "peg-
ging away," to use his own homely phrase
for his persevering and patient work. All this
is of the happiest augury for the future of
the Chartered Company, provided that he
remains the directing and controlling spirit of
the great enterprise which he launched in
1889, and has since then repeatedly saved
from shipwreck.

The shareholders of the Chartered Company
are probably perfectly well aware of the fact
that Mr. Rhodes is essential, if financial success is to be attained. Undoubtedly the Chartered Company requires to have at the helm
the very ablest financier living to cope with
the immense difficulties that immediately beset
it. With Mr. Rhodes it has temporarily lost
another valuable support of its stability, probably the most distinguished and far-sighted
captain of industry after Mr. Rhodes, in South
Africa—I mean Mr. Beit. If the shareholders

are wise they will not rest till they have got both of them back. The great practical abilities of both, as well as the influence of the proved success of their finance and organization in other ventures, are imperatively required to carry on developments which will tax even their energies to the utmost.

The colonists are, of course, fully aware that the leadership of Mr. Rhodes is absolutely essential to the progress of the country. Dutchmen and Englishmen alike joined, last summer, in the public meeting at Bulawayo, and demanded that Mr. Rhodes's resignation of his position on the Board of the Chartered Company should not be accepted; and the fact that they considered the matter simply from the standpoint of their own interests does not diminish the weight of their protest. Many of the Dutch settlers were burghers, fresh from the Transvaal; yet these Transvaalers, just settled in Rhodesia, were as eager to retain Mr. Rhodes as their head as were the Englishmen and Cape Colonists. This is significant, though it is not surprising; for no Englishman has got on so well with the Dutch, or done so much to remove racial animosity, as Mr. Rhodes. To live under his sway the Transvaal Boers are trekking across the Limpopo in ever-increasing numbers, and we may yet see the drain of burghers from the South African Republic give valuable aid to the settlement of the problem which the tyrannical Government of Pretoria, with its perpetual persecution of Englishmen, and its deliberate incitements to race-hatred, has succeeded in creating, with a view to maintain in power the jealous and corrupt Hollander clique, that administer the Republic for their own personal profit, and to the danger of South Africa.

Perhaps the most convincing evidence of this attitude of the settlers may be found in a leader published last Summer in that independent organ of Rhodesian Radicalism, *The Matabele Times*, which had been, till then, as bitter as Mr. Labouchere in its denunciations of the Chartered Company. The following extract contains a good deal of truth conveyed in sufficiently strong language :—

"Our expectations of a prosperous future are bound up in the continuance of government by the Chartered Company, and the Chartered Company is inseparably linked with the personality of Mr. Rhodes. The other members of the Board are, from the point of view of Rhodesians, as absolutely nonentities as are the shareholders. There was but one man among them, who displayed a higher sense of obligation than is involved in a commercial speculation; but one man who set himself to create a country that would be a worthy portion of the British Empire, as well as a dividend-producing region; but one man who devoted himself to the prosperity of a people, as against treating men and families as pawns in a stock-exchange game. With him eliminated, there may remain but a soulless company, capable of any Shylockian demand for prescriptive rights."

Of course this is less than justice to Earl Grey, who has laboured loyally with ability and self-denial in the administration of Rhodesia ; but there is a very large element of truth in the comparison between Mr. Rhodes and one or two of the other directors, which is, at any rate, the genuine expression of opinion in that section of the settlers which, till Mr. Rhodes himself came and lived among them, was as deeply discontented, and not to be reconciled to government from St. Swithin's Lane.

CHAPTER XV.

WE have now looked at Mr. Rhodes as a financier and a man, it is time that we should see him at work as a statesman. The two chief problems which demand solution in South Africa are, firstly, the reconciliation, with a view to gradual union, of the white races, the English and Dutch; and, secondly, the native question, how best to bring the education of true civilization to a rapidly increasing native population, which enormously outnumbers the whites. To the first of these, racial union, must be added its corollary, political union, the Federation of the various States of South Africa, so as to form a Union like that of the

United States or the Dominion of Canada. To see Mr. Rhodes at work upon these problems is to gain materials for an estimate of his achievements and his position as a statesman.

The best measure of Mr. Rhodes's success as to racial union, that is as to the reconciliation of the Dutch, is the fact that the faith of the Cape Dutch in the English Statesman has, to a marvellous extent, stood the enormous strain to which the catastrophe of the raid subjected it. No one except Mr. Rhodes himself believed this to be possible, and that he never doubted that the Dutch would return to their English leader and friend, shows how well he knew the reality of the reconciliation which he had effected. All his friends considered his political life over; he alone believed and stated that it had only begun. In his own person he had in the past gained the confidence of the Dutch Members of Parliament one by one. As they came to know him in his private life at Groote Schuur, they

learned to admire and trust him. The result
is, that not only has Mr. Hofmeyr and his
admirably worked caucus been unable to hold
the Dutch districts against the magnetism of
Cecil Rhodes (the welcome to Mr. Rhodes at
Wellington, Worcester, and the Paarl, testify
to this), but it was a Dutchman, not an Englishman, Mr. Bellingan, who maintained as
long ago as last March that even if Mr. Rhodes
had sent in Dr. Jameson, the one mistake could
not undo his previous great services to South
Africa; while it is Mr. Du Toit, a Dutchman
of Dutchmen, a father of the Afrikander Bond,
some time a prominent official of the Transvaal,
a foe of the Transvaal annexation and a friend
and active supporter of the retrocession, who
condemns the Transvaal Government's demand
for the abrogation of the Charter and the
removal of Mr. Rhodes from his great work in
South Africa.

Truly the utterances of these wise and statesmanlike Dutchmen, with their large liberality

and far-seeing good sense, make one ashamed of the yelping chorus of blatant Little Englanders, Radical freelances and stray Conservative cranks, which has clamoured for the new sensation of browbeating and insulting the great South African Statesman because of a single failure in his long series of distinguished services to the Empire.

The native question, the second of the two important problems which demand solution by colonial statecraft in South Africa, has been in large measure solved by Mr. Rhodes in his Glen Grey Act, which is intended to deal with the difficulties that have arisen in the Cape Colony with regard to the labour of the natives, their occupation of land, their indulgence in liquor, and the lack of occupation for their minds which the cessation of war— once their chief business in life—has brought.

In Rhodesia, of course, the sale of liquor to natives is strictly prohibited, and the plan for the Local Government of the tribesmen by the appointment of their feudal chiefs as paid officials of the Company, while they are also made responsible for the labour supply, is a masterly application of the gradual system of civilization commended by Dr. Wallace, and based on the principle that the transition from savagery to civilization must be gradual if it is to be satisfactory and permanent.

As regards the Cape Colony, the so far remarkably successful solution of the native question in the Glen Grey Act, which became law in 1894, demands some further description. The Act, called from the district of Glen Grey, had for its object to provide for the disposal of lands and for the administration of local affairs within the district above named and other proclaimed districts.

Overcrowding—a very real danger in the native territories—is provided against by a system of allotments, the succession, in order to prevent subdivision, descending by the law of primogeniture; while civic education is provided for by a system of local government by means of District Councils, which are empowered to raise taxes and expend the proceeds in local improvements.

The liquor traffic is controlled by local option, expressing itself through the District Council, and the labour tax is levied on male natives exclusively. "Every male native residing in the district, exclusive of natives in possession of lands under ordinary quit rent titles, or in freehold, who, in the judgment of the resident magistrate, is fit for and capable of labour, shall pay into the public revenue a tax of ten shillings per annum." The money thus levied is applied to maintain schools of industry; and so the idle native contributes to the promotion of industry in the next generation.

The distinctive characteristic of the Glen Grey Act, as may be seen from this brief sketch, is its practical and carefully designed educative influence, which make it by far the

most advanced and truly statesmanlike measure that has ever been brought to bear on the
difficult native question. Mr. Rhodes had long
before shown his sympathy with the natives,
and his desire that the ruling race, the white,
should raise the black race, as far as possible,
towards its own higher level of civilization.
The Glen Grey Act bids fair to accomplish
this desire, when its operation is extended to
embrace the various native territories.

After the Act had been in force six months
the Head of the Police went to Glen Grey, and
asked the jailer where the prisoners were.
The prison was generally crowded; now it
was empty. The jailer informed him that since
the Act had been in force he had had no
prisoners, for there had been no crime. The
men now go out and work instead of loafing
about and attending the Beer-Drinks, which
were the cause of all the crime in the district.

What the *pax Romana* was to the savage
tribes of Europe—a power to develop good

citizens as well as to stop war—that the *pax Britannica*, according to Mr. Rhodes's policy, is to be to the native races of South Africa. Its influence is to be not only protective but educative.

Of this beneficent work, which outweighs all that the Aborigines Protection Society have ever accomplished in South Africa, there is no account whatever taken by the enemies of Mr. Rhodes, whose detestation of the man and his work amounts to a positive mania.

The attacks of the hostile press continue undiminished, perhaps for the sake of consistency, though why so able and straight a man as Mr. Massingham should see so crooked it is hard to conjecture. The only explanation I can find is that he is absolutely misinformed as to the facts. The latest and most serious attack is that of callous indifference to the ill-usage of the natives. This charge is advanced with extraordinary force and virulence by the powerful pen of the one remarkable literary personage in South Africa. In "Trooper Peter Halket of Mashonaland," Mrs. Schreiner has produced a work of great literary ability dealing with the conduct of Mr. Rhodes and the Chartered Company towards the native races of Rhodesia.

She knew his record; she was acquainted with his acts and his policy, at the time when she ranked him so high. He is a better man now than then; yet now eulogy is exchanged for vituperation; and the statesman who has done so much to improve and educate these poor children, as he terms our dark-skinned fellow men in South Africa, is held up to opprobrium, as "death on niggers," as their uncompromising enemy and exterminator.

Can it be that, when Olive Schreiner imposed on the unknown Mr. Cronwright the distinction of her name, he imposed on her in return—brass for gold—his distorted views of Cecil Rhodes?

The question we have to ask ourselves as to

x

Mrs. Schreiner's "Trooper Peter Halket" is not whether it is written with consummate literary art, for that may be answered in the affirmative. It is a work of ability, but it is also a piece of personal invective of the most telling and terrible kind; and in the face of this fact the question we must ask ourselves is not "Is it beautifully written?" but "Is it true? Is it really true that Mr. Rhodes is a hater, oppressor and exterminator of 'niggers,'" as Mrs. Schreiner uses all her literary gifts to persuade her readers. The evidence obtainable is ample. He is a Statesman—turn to his legislation, the Glen Grey Act, designed to protect, educate, and elevate the black man. He is the head of the Chartered Company— turn to his great work in Rhodesia during the past year. He is an employer of black labour —turn to the record of his dealings with the natives he has employed in thousands for many years—you will find everything that can benefit them from recreation grounds and swimming baths to enforced total abstinence, and a manufactory of mineral waters as a substitute, carefully provided for. He is a man— turn to his own household, his black servants devoted to him, the sons of Lobengula at home in his house cared for, educated and treated as if they were the sons of their kind and fatherly protector.

Look at the evidence, and any fair-minded man or woman will be convinced that it is conclusive. Mr. Rhodes's humane and thoughtful treatment of the natives for years past proves his good-will towards them. Mrs. Schreiner's terrible indictment is absolutely without foundation.

The result of a careful examination of the evidence by a competent reader of "Peter Halket," who has no bias, will be that Mrs. Schreiner has written a work that shows consummate literary art, but has, at the same time, perpetrated a moral outrage by standing up as a false witness against a guiltless man. The aim of the book is ostensibly an attack on an individual for a high moral purpose; but because this attack is built on falsehood and inspired by long-nourished personal rancour and personal animosity, the book remains a monument of misused literary power; and Mrs. Schreiner, in producing one of the most powerful and persuasive literary indictments aimed against a public man, has produced one of the most deeply immoral books of our day. Never was there a sadder instance of the old saying, "Corruptio optimi pessima."

The introduction of the Divine figure of Christ has been objected to by many as blasphemous; but if the indictment had been true, the literary skill with which the Divine figure is introduced is so delicate and sure, that this objection would not hold. The deeper and sadder blasphemy of introducing the Spirit of Perfect Truth as a literary device to make plausible and effective a vindictive falsehood, is the real charge of blasphemy of which

Mrs. Schreiner, I regret to say, stands convicted.

There was plenty of trustworthy evidence available had Mrs. Schreiner chosen to obtain it. The evidence of such a man as the Rev. C. D. Helm, the senior missionary of the London Missionary Society in Matabeleland, who has lived over twenty years among the natives, long before the Chartered Company was thought of, is the kind of evidence that should have been sought by anyone desirous of knowing the truth. I obtained this evidence from him personally, and I have taken down from his dictation his statement, of which the following passage contains his actual words :—" In any case where there was any treatment of natives that I considered unfair, and I applied to the Chartered Company's officials, I have always found them ready to take up the case, and to act with the utmost vigour and impartiality in doing justice between black men and white. Of course there were cases of individual ill-treatment of black men by white prospectors. The most common of these, was the case of a prospector hiring boys by the moon (or month), and picking a quarrel with them just before the time was up, and beating the boys, who would then run away, and so lose their wages."

To meet this difficulty, I may observe, as Mr. Helm pointed out to me, Dr. Jameson formed a registry for native labour, and proclaimed the fact to all the Indunas— that all natives applying for work should register, when the Chartered Government would hold themselves responsible for wages, actually paying out the wages in case of dispute, and recovering from the white men afterwards if possible.

Mr. Helm continued his statement to me as follows :—" In my own experience, the Chartered Company used to get the best men they could as native Commissioners, and I have never known within the country where I have personal experience, of any case of illusage or injustice to natives by the Chartered Company's officials." I asked Mr. Helm was there any instance in his personal experience of forcible interference with native women by white men. He replied emphatically " No !" and he added : " There is no need for forcible interference with the black women : black women come freely to offer themselves to the white men—the difficulty is rather to keep them away." This difficulty has been very recently occupying the attention of the Chartered Company's officials, and cases of forcible interference with native women are non-existent, if for no better reason, that such compulsion is unnecessary. I have been obliged to touch on this unpleasant subject because Mrs. Schreiner has, with rare skill, made this charge one of the blackest in her indictment.

When I asked Mr. Helm to compare the state of Matabeleland before the occupation by the Chartered Company and since, he emphatically stated that "the change for the natives themselves is altogether for the better; there can be no two opinions about the matter."

The fact is Mrs. Schreiner knows nothing whatever, from personal enquiry, about the state of things in Mashonaland or Matabeleland. She has never been in the country at all.   She has never been, I believe, much farther North than Kimberley, many hundreds of miles from the country of which she writes. No doubt she may believe what she writes; but the basis of her terrible indictment of Mr. Rhodes and the Chartered Company is simply irresponsible hearsay. Whether it be a moral outrage or not to recklessly manufacture an indictment from such materials I leave it to the sense of fairplay in the English people to judge. It is well, however, that they should know that even after the occupation of Mashonaland by Mr. Rhodes and his Company, Olive Schreiner remained a personal friend and a fervent admirer of Mr. Rhodes. Students of human nature might be inclined to conjecture that her present attitude was to some extent the result of disappointment. On other grounds it is hard to explain.

I have not given half the evidence that might be adduced to prove that instead of being an enemy to, and exterminator of, the black man, Mr. Rhodes is his truest and most trusted friend in South Africa. I will find space for a little more. After Mr. Rhodes had made terms with the chiefs at the Indaba in the Matopos, he had still to get them accepted by the Imperial representative. Sir Richard Martin strongly objected to the mild and merciful terms made by Mr. Rhodes, and he at first refused to accept the settlement, insisting strongly on his own. His proposed settlement consisted of an immediate surrender, to be followed by the Indunas on his Black List coming down to be tried at Bulawayo. This Black List contained all the supposed rebel chiefs in the country, many of whom proved to be innocent, after inquiry. The chiefs, of course, would not entertain Martin's terms. They preferred the chance of being shot on a granite kopje in the Matopos to the probability of trying the strength of a hemp rope at Bulawayo.

Finding Sir Richard Martin obdurate, Mr. Rhodes warned him solemnly that if he recommenced hostilities against the natives he (Rhodes) would go into the Matopos, cast in his lot with the natives, and live among them; and further he warned the Imperial officer that if bloodshed took place it would be entirely his fault. Sir Richard Martin, who was of course not to blame, as he was merely carrying out his instructions, was at last reluctantly persuaded to let the merciful settlement have a trial. The result has been that since Mr. Rhodes made terms with them not a shot has been fired by the natives. They have loyally kept the compact they made with the Great White Chief, who had thus nobly earned his title of their Father by his generous protection of their lives and their interests. The natives, I believe, know of the struggle he had to save them and appreciate it. There was no weakness in the terms, for it was agreed that those natives found guilty of brutal murders of defenceless men, women and children, should be executed. Nor does Mr. Rhodes's title to be regarded as the Protector and Friend of the natives in Matabeleland end here. After the war was over the natives were in danger of starvation. Without crops and without cattle, the whole of the herds in Matabeleland having perished by the rinderpest, what were they to do? The Chartered Company had not at that time raised fresh capital, and the Directors could not see their way to face the necessary expenditure. Mr. Rhodes immediately supplied £50,000 out of his private purse, and with this money corn was at once purchased by Earl Grey, and the wants of the natives supplied.

At the least such proofs of the malignity and untruthfulness of Mr. Rhodes's assailants should enlighten the British public as to the real character of other attacks, which because he disdains to notice them, have been accepted as true. It would, of course, be too much to expect that his detractors, or even his countrymen in general, should at once realize and acknowledge the greatness of the man they have misrepresented or misunderstood, but they might at least acknowledge that he has amply earned the right to be called a truly humane man.

The union of the white races is the necessary first step to political union. The Federation of the States of South Africa, which has been the aim of Mr. Rhodes's policy for some years, must be brought about, as he fully understands, by a very gradual process, through which, racial feeling being got rid of, the more backward portion of the white population, the Boer farmers, must be educated, by experience, in the first place, of the advantages to their material interests of such measures as a customs union and a railway union.

The effects of the educating influence of his leadership are to be seen in the enlightenment and broad-minded wisdom which are now to be found in a large number of the Dutchmen of the Cape.

The well-meant attempts at Federation of Lord Carnarvon and Sir Bartle Frere failed, because they were imposed by the Imperial Government from without, and took no proper account of the state of local feeling and local unpreparedness, whereas under Mr. Rhodes's leadership, a genuine desire for Federation has been developed among the Colonists, aided by the practical influence of the advantages to the Cape Colony of a customs and railway union with Rhodesia, where in a few years' time a large and progressive population will be established.

In any estimate of Mr. Rhodes's achievements as a statesman, the great achievement
of his life, the acquisition for the Empire of
the most valuable portion of South Africa,
the immense territory which bears his name,
must not be forgotten.

He dominates the politics of South Africa
to-day largely because his greatness is identified with the expansion which has given
South Africa the possibility of a splendid
future, and has brought within range of practical realisation his dream of building up a
South African nation from the two white races,
for whose reconciliation and fusion he has
done so much.

His great achievement in colonial expansion is comparable only with the occupation of
North America by the Anglo-Saxon race, and,
were it not that our Government taught by
the past may be expected to avoid the errors
of the Government which was the cause of the
American revolution, the same impatience of

Government from Downing Street, which took from us the Greater Britain of America in the eighteenth century, might easily take from us the Greater Britain of Africa in our own day.

Under the controlling influence of Mr. Rhodes at the Cape and in Rhodesia there is no such danger to be feared ; for he understands the people of South Africa and their needs, being not only an Imperialist but also a South African by adoption and connection. His policy in Rhodesia, with its encouragement of immigration by Dutchmen of the Cape Colony and of the Transvaal and Free State, on perfectly equal terms with Englishmen from England and from the Cape Colony and Natal, is calculated to hasten the unification of South Africa, by welding together the white races by means of common commercial interests and united action for the defence as well as the development of their common country.

That great problem of South Africa, the consolidation and union of the white races, is

likely to be solved in Rhodesia before it is
solved elsewhere. This is what Mr. Rhodes
pointed out in his memorable speech at Port
Elizabeth, last December, and this is what
the Dutchmen, who are the vanguard of the
progress of their race, have perceived and are
acting upon. It is because he realises that
the future of South Africa depends upon the
presence, during the early stages of development, of a great leader to guide that development, that a Transvaaler like Du Toit throws
his weight into Rhodes's scale, feeling, as do all
to whom the progress of South Africa is dear,
that Cecil Rhodes is the one man fitted to
lead that progress, and at any cost his leadership must be secured.

At this point I would ask my reader to
look for a moment at the present from the
vantage ground of the future. When the
passage of another century has placed in
true perspective the events of our time, and
it is easy to judge of their relative impor-

tance, what will be in the estimation of the people of **England** the most noteworthy event of the latter half of the nineteenth century, the event whose consequences to the English race have been the most far-reaching and the most enduring? Not, one may safely say, the Crimean War, not the Indian Mutiny, not even the Arbitration Treaty with the United States, should that escape wreckers in the Senate. Rather, I think, the **most important event**, and, as it happens, the most advantageous, to the English race will be, **by** their general estimate, the acquisition for England in the last unoccupied Continent of the last unmarked territory where white men can thrive and **multiply, a territory in which** England would appear a province, the spacious regions of Rhodesia. And with the supreme importance of this expansion of the Empire and the race will be inevitably identified the greatness of the statesman by whom it was conceived and accomplished.

When the home legislation of a Gladstone and the foreign policy of a Salisbury are remembered only by the historian or the student of the period, the far-reaching consequences of the great work of Cecil Rhodes will keep his fame alive in the memory of the English race in England and in all the world. It will then be remembered that in the struggle of the Powers of Europe for the possession of the last virgin Continent, his was the far-sighted wisdom that had early seen the importance of the prize, his the patient resourcefulness that had prepared the plan of conquest, his the unresting energy and unbounded generosity that had made that plan effective. At that day, too, it is possible that the idea of the federation of the English-speaking race and the first step towards its realization may be traced to the same large-brained and long-sighted statesmanship, and it is more than probable that the building of a South African nation will acknowledge in him its architect.

What remains, however, little short of a certainty is the estimate, which **I have ventured to anticipate by a century,** of the relative importance of the English occupation of Rhodesia.   When the struggle for North America was going on between the European Powers in the last three centuries, there was a very imperfect conception **among** the statesmen of the time of the ultimate consequences of success in that struggle.   **Put South Africa in** the place of North America, and the **same** statement is as true of our own day.   The accomplished work of Mr. Rhodes bulks (I fear) smaller in the estimate, not only of the party politician, **but** of the public, than a military campaign **or** a new Franchise Bill.   This is as it has ever been **with** great events.   Contemporaries rarely perceive their significance. The superficial view of the moment takes more **account of** an insignificant accident like the Transvaal Raid, which will be clean forgotten in a decade, **than** of the occupation of the **best** of the Continent of Africa, which will be fertile of beneficial consequences when a century has passed away.

It requires no extraordinary effort of the imagination to picture another and not less valuable estimate—Rhodesia's estimate of its founder at the close of the twentieth century. Long before then—if I may anticipate the future—Rhodesia will be filled with a population of enterprising and progressive English blood, steadied by a useful dash of Conservative Dutch. The gold-mines of the territory will probably by that time have been worked out. But they will have served their purpose; enriched their owners, and increased the speed of colonization. The extensive coal-mines and mines of copper and the baser minerals will still be in full swing of prosperity. Towns of large size and high civilization will have sprung up, and Bulawayo and Salisbury will have their old-fashioned buildings where Rhodesians can examine the architecture of the last—that

is, the nineteenth century. Farmhouses and
villages will sprinkle for two thousand miles
in length, and a thousand in breadth, the
uplands of a greater England, largely engaged
in pastoral and agricultural pursuits.   Man-
sions of prosperous planters will look down on
the lakes Tanganyika, Moero, and Nyasa;
yachtsmen and rowing-men will frequent their
broad waters.   Steamers run by electricity will
ply on the Zambesi river, and the Victoria
Falls will supply power for lighting and other
purposes to numerous towns.   The South
African tourist will take his ticket at Bulawayo by the main line to Uganda, breaking
his journey for a trip on the steamboat service
of Nyasa or Tanganyika, just as the English
tourist to-day takes a ticket in London for Glas-
gow to visit the Scotch lakes.   The whole South
African nation, whatever their differences in
politics, will be united in a common sentiment,
in looking back with gratitude and admiration to the founder of their country, the states-

man acknowledged as the first cause of all this civilization and prosperity, whose *floruit* belongs to the beginning of their own century and the latter part of the preceding one.

That statesman will have gone to his long home; the unresting energy will be at rest, the strong brain dust; but his memory will live on among his people. The story of his strenuous career will animate and inspire the young man, and to have met him and spoken with him, will be the old man's proudest remembrance. The hero-worship of a great progressive people will centre round the career of that strong pioneer of progress, and a grave at Zimbabye and a lonely spot in the Matopo Hills, walled in by towering masses of granite, will be the shrines of many a patriotic pilgrimage.

With the judgment of the future before him, Cecil Rhodes can afford to ignore the petty detraction of purblind contemporaries. To the judgment of the future he can appeal with the certainty that it will applaud the unrivalled achievements of his energy, and estimate justly the whole patriotic purpose of his life. The expansion, of which he will be the acknowledged author, will then be seen to have been, not only an expansion of the Empire, but an expansion of the race, an expansion of English liberty, of English ideas and English principles. Men of that time who stand on the verge of the twenty-first century, as we on the verge of the twentieth, will wonder at the short-sighted judgment and narrow spirit that failed to recognise the greatness and the patriotism of the statesman and the man, that cavilled at his methods, and lightly esteemed the value of his accomplished work.

CHAPTER XVI.

JUDGED from the conventional standpoint of the admirer of elaborate and carefully studied oratory, the copious eloquence of a Gladstone, the perfectly chosen language of a Bright, the felicities of phrase and epithet of a Beaconsfield, Mr. Rhodes regarded merely as a speaker would certainly not be in the first rank. He is a practical statesman, who speaks only when it is necessary for purposes of statesmanship; not an orator or a rhetorician who seeks to electrify his hearers and produces his effects for show. Classical allusions and quotations he regards as mere ornamentation, and such ornamentation, like the gilding of fine language, is alien and distasteful to his intensely practical

mind with its clear outlook on the world as it
actually is. His speeches, however, have a
style of their own ; a style that is a revelation
of the man himself. This style is distinguished by a careless strength that permits
repetitions of the same word and the same
phrase, that prefers the homely and familiar
both in diction and simile to the strange and
exotic. He never writes a line even of his
weightiest speeches, he never makes a note
before he speaks ; he has pondered his subjects
long and deeply, he has arrived at his conclusions, which have for him the finality of complete conviction. He knows the thoughts and
arguments he intends to convey to his hearers,
and he does not concern himself with the manner
of conveying them. Enough for him if he can
make them clearly understand what he has in
his mind ; enough if he can make them carry
away the result of his solitary and intense
meditations. He loses the sense of his own
personal existence in the inspiring atmosphere

of the great ideas in whose company he loves to live his real and higher life.

Hence, when he gets up to speak, it is to bring forth the stores of a full mind. He is never in a hurry to rush through what he has to say. He has thought over it long, and he dwells upon it and expounds it deliberately. Sentence by sentence he unfolds his arguments, and drives home, by the steady enforcement of the logic of facts, the incontrovertible truth of his conclusions. He is intensely in earnest, and, while his gestures are at first somewhat stiff, when he warms with the unfolding of his subject they have the natural force and power of a man who forgets his own existence and his own interests in the conviction of the supreme importance to his hearers of the ideas and the policy he sets before them. All this gives a power of sheer reality to his speeches which fitly reflect the rugged reality of the man. He honestly believes with his whole mind and his whole heart in his ideas and his policy, and this gives him that rare power of convincing others with a final conviction, altogether different from the mirage of heated language with which a mere great orator or rhetorician surrounds and charms his audience for a moment; and sends them away, delighted indeed with the sensation of mental intoxication, but no wiser than they were; with no solid residuum of practical policy which will affect their views and influence their action. Mr. Rhodes believes that his ideas and his policy are of deep and far-reaching importance to his fellow-citizens, and he asks their confidence and co-operation in his work because he is convinced of its value to themselves.

The earnestness of the man is doubled in its effect by the immense physical and mental energy that vibrates through his words and gives colour and life to the simplest language. He has, as might be supposed, almost as much contempt for the arts of the trained orator as for the hair-splitting of the trained logician. His powerful reasoning faculty has nothing akin to the verbal subtleties of Gladstonian dialectics ; he strikes straight at the heart of his subject, and plain men can follow him and see that his success is not a conjurer's trick. That he has a rare power of convincing others, even the hardest men of the world, may be seen in such results as the conversion of Mr. Schnadhorst from Little Englandism to Imperialism, in the persuasion that brought over Mr. Barnato to join in the amalgamation, and actually to allow half a million of De Beers money to be poured out to smooth the way of expansion to the North.

These instances, it may be said, are not instances of his persuasive power as a speaker— rather of his power as a talker ; but the truth is, he talks to the largest audience as simply and unaffectedly as he talks to a single man. His speeches, with their wealth of anecdote and reminiscence, with their easy colloquialisms

and homely similes, are nothing else but his
conversation on a large scale. The same convincing power that inspires the one inspires the
other. It is the magnetic force of his strong
personality, full of great ideas, and absolutely
in earnest, that counts in a speech to the many
as in a talk to one or two. It would be a mistake to suppose he had no power over words.
In his speeches, as in his conversation, he has
the faculty of putting the essence of an argument into one strong phrase. Occasionally,
too, his invective is as personal and keen-
edged as Beaconsfield's. Such was his description of Mr. Labouchere as a "cynical sybarite,"
or better still, of the Lord Chief Justice's
attitude towards the raid as "unctuous rectitude."

But still the fact remains that it is the
weight of his massive personality that makes
the unconscious revelation of himself in his
speeches so effective in its influence on those
who read, as well as those who hear his

words. He is, as I have pointed out, a man of great ideas, who lives his inner life in company with great ideas. He is also a man of imagination, with a range of vision which is very rare. Where the horizon of an English party leader is at the utmost bounded by the life of a Parliament, or more commonly by the duration of a session, Mr. Rhodes's horizon extends into the centuries that have still to come.

His generalisations have the immense range and the extraordinary accuracy that it is difficult to ascribe to anything but genius, genius in statesmanship of the very highest order. The unification of South Africa is the immediate ideal which he considers as lying within his own power to make an accomplished reality; but that is only a step towards the larger unification of which he dreams, in which England and England's Colonies shall all be included in a vast federation, proceeding out of a commercial union of the English race.

Further yet, in a far distant future, when his life-work is done, his imagination already sees the United States federated with England and England's Colonies in a unification so vast that it will govern and guide the progress of the world. The immensity of this forecast of the future lays it open to the charge of Utopianism; but, like all Mr. Rhodes's imaginative ideas, it has a solid basis of facts, of which these alone are worth remembering: that sixty-six years ago English was spoken by eighty-five millions less persons than now, and that while the English-speaking race has increased eighty-five millions the rest of the races of Europe have increased one hundred and twenty-five millions only. The governing race is also becoming the dominant race in wealth, progress, power, as well as numbers. The federation, then, of the English-speaking race, the reign of industrialism and peace, is the far horizon of his political vision; and so the expansion of the British Empire, a step towards this high ideal, means to him the extension of British institutions, of British freedom and self-government, over the largest possible extent of the habitable earth. His work in South Africa is the realisation of this ideal in a single continent. Believing, thus, with his whole heart and mind in all that the extension of the British Empire means to the British race, and through them to mankind, his patriotism, I might say his Imperialism, as it is the strongest conviction of his mind, is also the deepest sentiment of his heart, the single over-mastering motive that rings through his speeches as it has swayed and sways his life. This is the real explanation of the madness, as it has seemed to many of his friends, of risking his whole great position and prospects on the uncertain result of the effort to secure to the English population in the Transvaal their rights as citizens. The inevitable result of success was, he saw, South African unification.

For the sake of all that the British Empire

means to him; for the sake of the Federation of all South Africa under a Federal flag, the British flag, at Cape Town, he took the enormous risk, and for this alone.

The extracts from Mr. Rhodes's speeches, though the colossal inaccuracy of the reporters in South Africa somewhat mars the effect, will help any thoughtful reader to understand the secret of his power over men as a speaker, better, probably, than any analysis of that power can.

First of the speeches I have selected may be placed the speech before the Annual Congress of the Afrikander Bond in 1891. Mr. Rhodes had just returned from England, and early in his speech pointed out the fact of the reconciliation he had effected between the aims of the Afrikander Bond, and the sentiment of loyalty to the Empire; a speech, of course, unknown to Mr. J. Mackenzie.

"I think in the past," he said, "it would have been considered an extraordinary anomaly that one who possessed the confidence of the Queen herself, should have been able to show that at the same time he felt most completely and entirely, that the objects and aspirations of the Bond were in complete touch and concert with fervent loyalty to Her Majesty the Queen."

He went on to say that he came to the Congress of the Bond—

"Because I wished to show that there is nothing antagonistic between the aspirations of the people of this colony and their kindred in the Mother Country, provided always that the Old Country recognizes that the whole idea of the colonies and of the colonial people, is that the principle of self-government must be observed and acted upon in full, and that the capacity of the colony be admitted to deal with every internal matter that may arise in the country. The principle must be recognized in the Old Country that people born and bred in this colony are much better capable of dealing with various matters than people who have to dictate seven thousand miles away."

After speaking at some length of the principles of the Bond, and of their feeling to the northern development, he went on,

"I have no hesitation in stating that I have every confidence in the future of these new northern territories, and I can also state that I shall never abandon my object. These territories possess a sufficient amount of wealth to demand, in time, the principle of self-government. A change must then occur from the chartered system of government to the Imperial system of self-government, and from self-government to a system of union with Cape Colony."

Again, he went on,

"If there was anything that induced me to take the position of Prime Minister, it was the fact that I had resolved in my mind that we should extend to the Zambesi. I thought it a grand idea to work for the development of the Zambesi regions, and at the same time to remain in touch and in concert with the people of Cape Colony. I mention this whilst proposing the toast of the Bond, because the sentiment and object of the Bond are Union (although you have not stated it in so many words) south of the Zambesi. I say south of the Zambesi, because I have discovered that up to there white human beings can live ; and wherever in the world white human beings can live, that country must change inevitably to a self-governing country. There, Mr. President, is an extraordinary flight of the imagination, that there must be a self-governing white community up to the Zambesi in connection with the United South. What has been the case in other parts of the world ? Look at the enormous development and union of the United States. That union did away with differential tariffs of all sorts, and gave to America a united people."

*   *   *   *   *

" The mistake that has been made in the past is the idea that a Union can be made in half-an-hour, whether rightly or wrongly, for the good of the country. It took me twenty years to amalgamate the diamond mines. That amalgamation was done by detail, step by step, attending to every little matter in connection with the people interested ; and so your Union must be done by detail, never opposing any

single measure that can bring that Union
closer, giving up even some practical advantage for proper union; educating your children
to the fact that that is your policy, and that
you will and must have it, telling it to them
and teaching it to them in your households,
and demanding that they shall ever hand on
the idea. In connection with this question I
may meet with opposition, but if I do, I shall
never abandon it. I have obtained enormous
subscriptions in order to found a teaching
University in Cape Colony. I will own to
you why I feel so strongly in favour of that
project. I saw at Bloemfontein the immense
feeling of friendship that all members had for
the Grey Institute, where they had been educated and from which they had gone out into
the world. I said to myself, if we could get
a teaching University founded in Cape Colony,
taking the people from all parts at the age of
eighteen to twenty-one, they would go back
tied to one another by the strongest feeling
that can be created, because the period in
one's life when one indulges in friendships
that are seldom broken is from eighteen to
twenty-one. Therefore, if we had a teaching

residential University, these young men would go forth into all parts of South Africa prepared to make the future of the country, and in their hands this great question of Union could safely be left."

This speech sets forth his ideal of South African Union, and suggests one of the practical means towards its realisation. The chief means, however, towards that end, which he has kept before him throughout his political life, is, in his opinion, the accomplished work of Northern expansion which he showed in his speech at Port Elizabeth last December to be bringing that end nearer by teaching union in a practical way to men of the Cape Colony, of Natal, of the Free State, and of the Transvaal Republic, who had come up to Rhodesia as settlers, and become practically a united people with common interests and aims in the work of the development and defence of a common country. This is no recent discovery of Mr. Rhodes's. He is not one of those statesmen who discover the trend of circumstances after the event. As long ago as 1888 he expressed this view to a Griqualand West audience before the Charter had been sought or obtained, when shrewd politicians could not help smiling at his Utopian imaginings.

"The extraordinary mixture of a crown colony, such as Natal, of republics, such as the Transvaal and the Free State, of a large native territory whose inhabitants are alien to the whites in race and sentiments, of a self-governing colony such as the Cape, divided in itself owing to racial divisions—all this seemed a problem impossible to deal with; but I felt that there are keys to every puzzle, and I came to the conclusion—and I have the courage to challenge anyone to deny it—that the key of the puzzle lay in the possession of the interior, at that time an unknown quantity. I hope that if any of you think I am showing a personal egotism, you will excuse it, from the fact that in a humble way I have been mixed up with the politics of the interior during the last four years; and these politics, I contend, will be in

the future most intimately connected with the
settlement of the South African Question; for
I believe that whatever State possesses Bechuanaland and Matabeleland will ultimately
possess South Africa. * * * *

"The possession of the interior by the Cape
Colonists, was in my opinion, then as now, the
means by which the Union of South Africa
under the British flag was to be brought about.
Recognising every debt of gratitude to the
Imperial Government, they (the Cape Colonists)
were fully prepared to retain the principle of
joint responsibility in respect to Imperial
defence; but in respect to the internal management of these territories they claim the principle of Home Rule. I have little more to
add; the politics of South Africa are in a nut-
shell. Let us leave the Free State and the
Transvaal to their own destiny. We must
adopt the whole responsibility of the interior.
We must propose a Customs Union on every
possible occasion, but we must always remember
that the gist of the South African question lies
in the extension of the Cape Colony to the
Zambesi. If you are prepared to take that,
there is no difficulty in the future. We must

endeavour to make those who live with us feel that there is no race distinction between us, that, whether Dutch or English, we are combined in one object, the object being the Union of the States of South Africa, without abandoning the Imperial tie."

A very good specimen of Mr. Rhodes's more colloquial style is to be found early in a speech of his delivered at a banquet to him at Cape Town in January, 1894. He is speaking of his idea of expansion to the North, which has been the guiding star of his political life from the very first.

"I remember, and it is an amusing recollection, that I used almost daily to see your late Governor, Sir Hercules Robinson. I had to deal with the acquisition of Bechuanaland, which is our frontier district. I had to deal with the expansion of the Protectorate which, if I remember right, was latitude 22°; and I remember so well that in my discussions with your late Governor he was good enough to say, ' Well, I think that is enough,' and the only reply I made to him was, 'Do come with me and look at the Blockhouse on Table Mountain.' I used that expression to him, and then I said, 'These good old people, two hundred years ago, thought that Blockhouse on Table Mountain was the limit of their ideals —but now let us face it to-day. Where are we? We are considerably beyond the Vaal River, and supposing that those good people were to come to life again to-day, what would they think of it and their blockhouses?' Then I said, 'Sir, will you consider during the temporary period you have been representative of Her Majesty in this Colony, what you have done? we are now on latitude 22°.' It was amusing when he said to me, 'And what a trouble it has been!' He said to me, 'But where will you stop?' and I replied, 'I will stop where the country has been claimed.' Your old Governor said, 'Let us look at the map,' and I showed him that it was the Southern border of Tanganyika. He was a little upset. I said that the great Powers at home marked the map and did nothing; adding, 'Let us try to mark the map, and we know that we shall do something.' 'Well,' said Sir Hercules Robinson, 'I think you should be satisfied with the Zambesi as a boundary.' I replied, 'Let us take a piece of note-paper and let us measure from the Block-house to the Vaal River, that is the individual effort of the people.' 'Now,' I said, 'let us measure what you have done in your tempo-rary existence, and then we will finish up with your measuring my imaginations. . . . .' We took a piece of note-paper and measured the efforts of the country since the Dutch occu-pied and founded it. We measured what he had done in his life, and then we measured my imaginations ; next we took the lines on the note-paper, and His Excellency, who is no longer with us, said, ' I will leave you alone.' Well, the idea progressed ; and His Excellency gave me a free hand, but he claimed from me a certain action when he considered that he had strained the responsibilities of Her Majesty's Government to the fullest extent. He claimed that I should take an obligation when we got to the 22nd degree of latitude, which was then the boundary of Khama's country. It is unnecessary for me to tire you with a statement of the endless negotiations which ensued. I found **myself** with the responsibility as far as the Zambesi, that is in so far as the High Commissioner of the Colony, and far beyond in so far as the Foreign Office, was concerned. I took upon myself these responsibilities because I thought it would come out all right. You must remember that in those days everyone was against me—you must remember that, when I pointed out to the House, as an individual member, that the Hinterland must be preserved, I could not get a single vote—I could not get a single vote, and I had to continue this in spite of every difficulty. I am now referring to twelve years of my life—twelve years as an individual member, and twice as a Minister of the Crown. But it came out all right. I have found out one thing, and that is, that if you have an idea, and it is a good idea, and if you will only stick to it, you will come out all right. I made the seizure of the interior a paramount thing in my politics, and made everything else subordinate, and if there are some of you who at times considered that any action of mine, as a member of the House, was such as you could not agree with, I can only say in reply that probably in

any case I should have to differ from you, but
frequently the paramount object weighed with
me as the supreme, and I knew that Africa was
the last uncivilized portion of the Empire or the
world and that it must be civilized, and that
those who lived at the healthy base with the
energy that they possess, would be the right
and proper individuals to undertake the civilization of the back country. I will not tire you
with what occurred. I was fortunate in being
in the position which falls to few; to have an
idea, and to be able to call upon funds in
support of that idea."

He went on to describe at great length and
in detail the reasons for the first war with the
Matabele and the overthrow of the savagely
cruel tyranny of Lobengula and his marauding
Impis, which meant the gift of peace and
safety to hundreds of thousands of inoffensive
and unwarlike natives, who had lived before
in terror of the Matabele raids.

A passage in which he dealt with the well-
meant but ignorant misrepresentations and

attacks of the Aborigines' Protection Society upon the Chartered Company is worth giving here.

"When the Charter was granted, Her Majesty sent a letter to the King, telling him to recognize the Charter; but at the same time there was a breakfast given by the Aborigines' Protection Society, and they gave a letter also that the King should work his gold himself, and that he should not give it to any adventurers. The two letters arrived together. The King made careful examination, and he found, unfortunately, that at the breakfast they were all gentlemen with white hair, and he said, 'It is clear to me that Her Majesty has given a nominal letter in favour of Rhodes, but her old councillors have sent another.' This was in terms of native ideas, and the King did his duty; and do you know what that duty was? He went promptly and murdered the man who had witnessed the concession, and seventy of his people, men, women, and children. When remonstrated with afterwards he said, 'Oh, but the old greybeards told me to do it'—the old greybeards being the Aborigines' Protection Society."

After a very telling criticism of the unscrupulous attacks of Mr. Labouchere, in which an extremely happy parallel is drawn from the Roman Empire two thousand years ago, Mr. Rhodes went on to deal with the Little Englander's policy from the standpoint of a practical man of business.

"They (*i.e.*, the electors) require to be educated; they require to be told that the Little England which he advocates is destruction to their industry; that England is a very small country with a very large population, which has lived during the last hundred years by working up raw product and then giving it to the world; that the world, which is very clever, has suddenly discovered that through giving to the world the raw product, when manufactured, England has got control of the world, and to sum it up shortly, the world by protective and prohibitive tariffs says, 'We will have nothing to do with England.' If

I could put before you a simile—and it appeals to every one of you, because we are all a sporting community—it is just as if a cricket eleven, we will say for the county of Yorkshire, beat everybody else. The neighbouring counties get nervous and frightened, and say we will handicap you with fourteen men when we play, and then they say we will handicap you with sixteen men, and then they say we won't play with you at all. That is just the habit of the world. It has nothing to do with us here, the politicians of England do not conceive the situation, but that is why the Little England is hopeless. If England was a country like the United States, with a huge expanse of territory, it might enter upon such a career, but with an entirely small island, almost at the present moment a workshop, its future depends upon its relations with the external world. And those relations depend upon its relations with the colonies of South Africa, of Australia, of Canada, and of the rest of the world. No politician has yet hit that idea. If the world as a whole hit on prohibitive tariffs against the mother country, what would occur? I will give you one more simile. The land cannot afford the support of forty millions, and they would be exactly in the position of a ship out of which the provender had been taken, and yet you leave the rats. The food having been exhausted, there is only one solution, and that is to eat themselves. . . . The United States are shutting us off with prohibitive tariffs ; France, Russia, almost every civilized power in the world, is doing it. They say they will not play cricket with us, and the only solution is to make arrangements to play cricket with your Colonies."

At a later point in this long and thoughtful speech, lighted up with big ideas, crammed with convincing facts, and driven home, as is his wont, with the homeliest and yet happiest analogies expressed in the most colloquial language, Mr. Rhodes dealt in his masterly way with the question of the union of South Africa.

" The future to me is a steady attempt to apply whatever we have in the old portion of

South Africa to those new estates which we have obtained—if you will let me use the personal pronoun, which I have obtained—and wait for the future, for no one will remove from me the idea that the day will come when there will be one system south of the Zambesi. With full affection for the flag I have been born under, and the flag I represent, I can quite understand the sentiment and feeling of a Republican who has created his independence, and values that before all; but I can say fairly that I believe in the future that I can assimilate this system which I have been connected with, with the Cape Colony, and it is not an impossible idea that the neighbouring republics, retaining their independence, should share with us as to certain general principles. If I might put it to you, I would say—the principle of tariffs, the principle of railway connection, the principle of appeal in law, the principle of coinage, and, in fact, all those principles which exist at the present moment in the United States, irrespective of the local assemblies which exist in each separate State in that country. I fully recognize—excuse me wandering into this—that even if so far as the flag were concerned we were one united people, it would be better in so far as concerns the gold of Johannesburg, and the coffee, tea, and sugar of Natal, that there was a local Assembly dealing with those matters; and whether that local Assembly happens to be under our flag or whether it is not, surely it is not a very high conception to think that as to general questions—those broad questions of railways, tariffs, coinage, and dealing with the natives—we should have a unanimous policy.

"And that is the future in so far as the special questions that I have been dealing with, that will have to be assimilated with the Government of the Cape Colony by degrees; in so far as regards its laws, railways, and tariffs.

"When you ask for immediate movement in these matters, I think of the warning of Sir Bartle Frere: 'You must never hurry anything. You must take step by step in accordance with the feeling and sentiment of the people as a whole. You may be more progressive in one of the cities of a country, but if you are wise, you will consider the relations of that city with the whole. Never hurry and hasten anything.' I remember, in the impetuosity of my youth, I was talking to a man advanced in years, who was planting—what do you think? He was planting oak-trees, and I said to him, very gently, that the planting of oak-trees by a man advanced in years seemed to me rather imaginative. He seized the point at once and said to me, 'You feel that I shall never enjoy the shade.' I said, 'Yes,' and he replied, 'I had the imagination, and I know what that shade will be, and at any rate no one will ever alter those lines. I have laid my trees on certain lines; I know that I cannot expect more than to see them beyond a shrub; but with me rests the conception and the shade and the glory.' And so I would submit to you the idea that many of us have conceptions, and we may also have the frank conception that in our temporary existence the results cannot be known; but we can work slowly and gradually for those results which may come beyond our temporary existence; and it is satisfactory to feel that you may found the lines in the same way that I saw the pleasure of this individual, who was laying the lines of his oak-trees.

*　　　*　　　*　　　*　　　*

"My motives have been assailed. I have many enemies, and they have insinuated many reasons; but they do not understand yet the full selfishness of my ideas; and I will take you into my confidence and say this to you, that I have a big idea that I wish to carry out, and I know full well the reward: the reward is one which is the highest that a human being can obtain, and that reward is the trust, the confidence, and the appreciation of my fellow citizens."

This admirable speech, with its revelation of Mr. Rhodes's far-reaching outlook over life, as well as the statement of his statesmanlike solution of the labour problem in England, ends with a passage which gives an instructive example of the crimes of the newspaper reporters against a speaker who has had more ill-usage at their hands than, probably, any other speaker living. The central point of this admirable conclusion is obviously the word "selfishness," after which, as anyone might conjecture, and as I have ascertained from one who was present, Mr. Rhodes paused at the word "ideas," and pausing, raised to the highest the suspense of his hearers as to what "the selfishness of my ideas" might be. Will it be believed that this word "selfishness" appears in many, if not most, versions of the speech as "unselfishness," though the change destroys the sense, and makes Mr. Rhodes a prig, which no one, however prejudiced against his policy and character, would accuse him of being.

And here I may observe that all Mr. Rhodes's speeches suffer more than the speeches of any other statesman, with whose work I am acquainted, from the fact that there is not a line of any of them written, and their maker, in his large carelessness as to petty details and his dependence on great work rather than fine words, absolutely refuses to revise a single line. The fact is that even in the Chartered Company's reports the speeches are left in places a mixture of the third person and the first, the present tense and the past—obviously the result of the reporting. This independent attitude is very rare, as any one knows who has seen how carefully our politicians compose their speeches beforehand, and how much trouble they take to hand type-written or printed copies to the reporters, so that the best possible form of the speech (a form very commonly altogether superior to the spoken speech) meets the public eye. It is useless to wish that Mr. Rhodes would take the same trouble, but really he goes too far in his carelessness and is utterly unjust to himself in letting all the errors and all the solecisms springing from the ignorance, the imperfect hearing or imperfect comprehension of the reporters remain uncorrected to injure, though they may not spoil, the effect. I should greatly like to restore the text of Mr. Rhodes's speeches, but that requires the assistance of the speaker, and this one need not hope to obtain.

CHAPTER XVII.

As Secretary for Native Affairs, an office he held with the Premiership, Mr. Rhodes, to whom any difficult problem of statesmanship is as a magnet to iron, attempted in 1894, when he had not yet been a year Native Minister, to deal thoroughly with perhaps the most important problem of South Africa, the Native Question. He moved the second reading of the Glen Grey Bill in a speech of great length, in which he proposed a large scheme of reform, and showed a sympathy with the blacks and a care for their interests not common in South Africa. I cannot refrain from quoting some passages from this speech—one of those in which appears unconsciously the genuine philanthropy which he hides, when among the cynical, under a veneer of cynicism.

"There is a general feeling that the natives are a distinct source of trouble and loss to the country. I take a different view. . . . . The proposition I have to put to the House is that I do not feel that the effect of having one million of natives in the country is a reason for any serious anxiety. Properly directed and properly looked after, the natives would be a great source of assistance and wealth. . . . . It happened that at the re-arrangement of the Cabinet I was given charge of the natives, and naturally what faced one was the enormous extent of the problem. I find that by the tacit consent of the House the Native Minister is practically left to deal with the interests of something like a million of natives. It also happens that in another direction on this side of the Zambesi I am responsible for another half million, and I believe a further half million beyond the Zambesi. . . . . That means a very great personal responsibility, and the question at present uppermost in my mind is: 'What is the present state of these people?' I find that you have certain locations for them where, without any right or title to the ground, they are herded together. I find that they are multiplying to such an enormous extent that these locations or areas have become too small for them. . . . . The old diminution of war and pestilence does not occur; good government defends them from that, and the result is an enormous multiplication of children. . . . . The question thus presents itself to us: firstly, the land will not continually provide for the increase. Secondly, you have provided nothing for them to occupy their minds with in place of the old system of making war between each other. Thirdly, you have placed canteens in their midst, and naturally a man who has nothing to do and is idle turns to the canteen. Fourthly, you leave them in those great preserves and do not teach them the dignity of labour. They live about in sloth and laziness and never go out to work. . . . The question is how to keep the minds of the natives employed. Friends of the natives will not hear of their minds being employed in any other capacity than in electing members of

Parliament. . . . However, I take up a much humbler position, and think you might first allow these children, just emerged from barbarism, to manage their own local affairs. Having proposed that they should form councils, I would let them, so that it should not be a farce, tax themselves, and I would give them funds to spend in building bridges, and making roads, and planting forests. I have not been asked by any member of Parliament to do that; but certain natives I met in the Transkei said they did not care about the Parliamentary question, but wanted their minds employed on local matters. They said they had nothing now to do but grow mealies and think of mischief, and asked, could not we give them work in matters they were interested in?"

At a later period in his speech he said,

" I know the curse of liquor. Personally at the diamond-fields I have assisted in making ten thousand of these poor children hard-working and sober. They were now in compounds healthy and happy. In their former condition

the place was a hell upon earth. Therefore
my heart is thoroughly with the idea of re-
moving liquor from the natives."

     *   *   *   *   *

"The next object of the bill comes under
the head of labour tax. I am told that this is
slavery. Various papers in the colony take it
that all would have to pay the labour tax
whether they work or not. That is not the
case. What I find is this—that we must give
some gentle stimulant to those people to make
them go out and work. The position at present is the following :—There are a large
number of young men in these locations who
are like the younger sons at home, or rather
the young men about town. They go to beer-
drinks, or to their brothers or fathers for food,
and so they remain in these large areas and
never do a stroke of work. I want to apply a
gentle stimulant to them. The result would
be this : when a young man was required to
pay ten shillings labour tax, he would run to
his brother. A brother would always give
him food, but when it came to putting his
hand in his pocket, he would say, 'I have not
got it, you must go to work.' That is the

direct stimulant to make these young men work. Their present position is similar to that of the young man about town, who loafs about the club in the day, dresses himself up for parties and afternoon tea in the evening, eats and drinks too much, and probably finishes up with immorality. . . . They are not in a position to marry, because they have not the cows; but they go to the beer-drinks and cause trouble in the domestic circle. . . . Now, in reference to this much-abused labour tax, it must be remembered that the whole of the funds are to be used for their own benefit. I propose to devote the money to industrial schools and to giving instruction in useful trades. To put it in other words, I might say it is intended that the neglect of labour should provide the funds for instruction in labour."

And he ended thus :—

" Indeed you may say this is a native bill for South Africa. You are sitting in judgment on Africa at this moment. I have merely submitted to the House my ideas on the question. It is a proposition submitted to

provide them with district councils ; it is a
proposition submitted to employ their minds
on simple questions in connection with local
affairs ; it is a proposition to remove the
liquor pest ; and last, but not least, by the
gentle stimulant of the labour tax you will
remove them from the life of sloth and laziness.
You will teach them the dignity of labour,
and make them contribute to the prosperity of
the State, and make them give some return
for our wise and good government."

This Glen Grey Act brings before us the
immense energy and philanthropy of the man,
who, with the weight upon him of the development of the North and the ordinary business of
Premier of the Cape Colony, must needs attempt,
simply because he felt the great responsibility
of the condition and the prospects of the
natives, the most difficult problem in South
Africa, the civilisation, by the educative influence of local self-government and industrial
education, of the enormous native population
of Cape Colony. The check on the liquor

traffic which he provided is of the nature of local option, with the same evident intention of elevating these poor children, as—with a compassionate touch—he calls the natives, to a higher level of humanity by teaching them to help themselves. His own maxim, a precept perpetually enforced by his practice, "The great secret of a happy life is work," is the motive of that part of the Act (Part iv. 33—36), which deals with labour and endeavours to supply a gentle but much needed stimulus to the idle and indolent Kaffirs. Assuredly the Glen Grey Act, which, but for the labour clause, would have passed into law not without considerable difficulty, owing to the dislike to it of the vineyard owners of the West, whose staple is brandy, is the work of a true statesman, one who looks far into the future, and tempers paternal legislation with the educative influence of self-government, giving to the native District Councils the spending on public works of the money they are empowered to raise.

We are far too apt to confuse parliamentary oratory with statesmanship. In the far-sighted practical wisdom of his legislation Mr. Rhodes has a much better title to the rarely deserved reputation of being a great statesman than if he possessed the most astonishing eloquence that ever was heard at Westminster.

To give Mr. Rhodes's speeches without his speeches concerning the Chartered Company would not be so bad as to present the play of *Hamlet* without the protagonist; but would certainly be to challenge criticism for inexplicable omission.

From a speech made at the Second Annual Meeting of the Chartered Company in November, 1892, I take the following passage, which puts very convincingly the then unnoticed fact that extension of British territory is far more to the interest of the masses than of the classes, being, as Mr. Rhodes concisely observed, a question of pleasure to the classes, a question of life to the masses.

"The idea that the taking up of the uncivilized portions of the world is to the advantage of the classes is erroneous; the proceeding
is entirely to the advantage of the masses.
The classes could spend their money under any
flag, but the poor masses had no money to
spend on these speculations—these gold and
silver mines; they could only look to other
countries in connection with what they produced, in connection with their factories and
their work. The point I desire to impress upon
the masses is that, instead of the world going
all right, it is going all wrong for them.
Cobden had his idea of free trade for all the
world, but that idea has not been realised.
The whole world can see that we can make the
best goods in this country, and the countries
of the world therefore established against us,
not protective tariffs, but prohibitive tariffs.
Let us take the case of 'the bone of our bone
and flesh of our flesh,' the Yankees. What is
the meaning of the McKinley tariff? It does
not mean that they wanted a revenue, but that
they desire to prohibit any trade with this
country. Perhaps one of the most humorous
things that ever happened was the Chicago

Exhibition. I said to my colleagues at the Cape, 'Are you aware that we are showing in a country that has declared that it does not want to trade with any other country? Are you aware that we are spending £10,000 to exhibit in Chicago? 'Brother Jonathan' is going to be very pleased to see us, but as soon as his exhibition is over he is going to lock his doors against us, and he does not wish to see us again until there is another Chicago Exhibition —for the glory of 'Brother Jonathan.'

"Our statesmen talk a great deal about Home Rule. When this matter is arranged, it will probably be found that it all settled down to a mere delegation of local affairs, hitherto managed at St. Stephen's, to district assemblies, and we shall all wonder afterwards why we talked so much about it. Another section of the people is agitating very considerably about a reduction in the hours of labour to eight, without realizing that this is impossible unless they can establish a ring fence round that portion of the habitable globe which agrees to work for eight hours only, with a tariff against the rest which work for more than eight hours. The question of the day, however, is the tariff question, and no one tells the people anything about it. I wonder if the Member for Northampton, for instance, has ever told his constituents that the world is trying to shut their boots out. That is the tendency of the whole habitable globe. It seems to be forgotten in talking about these islands that there are 36 millions of people, and that the islands will only produce sufficient to support 6 millions, the other 30 millions being entirely dependent on the trade of the world. I maintain that the first duty of statesmen is to keep this question open, even to the extent of retaliatory tariffs.

"I read the newspapers frequently, but I never see anything about this question. I know full well, as many of those present do, that if President Harrison's policy is continued by the Yankees, they will absorb Canada, make reciprocal arrangements with South America, and declare the New World to be self-supporting. I want to show the masses that the question of the day for them is the tariff question, and this country is the last country that should abstain from dealing with it. It is very different with France, with its enormous agricultural wealth and the nature of the people, and it is very different with the United States also, but with this country it is the question, and the whole question. How does this apply? Let us take the case of this much abused Africa. Our friend of Northampton calls it nothing but jungle. I would call it Cinderella. It has made marvellous development. If we take two parts of Africa only, Egypt and South Africa, we shall find that these two places alone are sending to this country exports amounting to £20,000,000. Egypt has been turned into a self-supporting country, and if England retires from it chaos will ensue. The interest on its debt would not be paid, its exports would not be made to this country, and this country would not send its goods in return. Perhaps I am rather tiring the meeting, but I desire to point out to you that it is your duty, wherever and whenever you can, to impress upon the masses that this question of keeping control of the outer world is a matter of pleasure to the classes, but that it is a question of life to the masses."

From the speech to the Chartered Shareholders at the Cannon Street Hotel, in
January, 1895, I select the following passages,
which are generally interesting as showing the
range of the great statesman's ideas on a
matter that concerns England rather than
South Africa.

"We have received throughout the complete
support of the Cape people, who, recognising
that it was too great an undertaking for themselves to enter upon, were glad that we undertook it, and they look upon it as their hinterland,
as, remember, we shall pass from the position
of Chartered administration to self-government when the country is occupied by white
people, especially by Englishmen, because if
Englishmen object to anything it is to being
governed by a small oligarchy. They will
govern themselves. We must look therefore
to the future of Charterland, I speak of ten
or twenty years hence, as self-government, and
that self-government very possibly federal
with the Cape government. Then, when we
think of the political position, we have also

to consider the English people, and I may say we have received the very heartiest support from the English public, with a few exceptions—possibly from ignorance, possibly from disappointment—and I think possibly from utter misconception. I remember while coming home I was sitting on board ship, and some one handed me the *Daily Chronicle*, in which I read the following:—'Not a single unemployed workman in England is likely to secure a week's steady labour as a result of the forward policy in South Africa.' What is the reply to that? I do not reply with a platform address about 'three acres and a cow,' or the 'social programme;' but I make a practical reply, and say what we have done. We have built 200 miles of railway—the rails all made in England, and the locomotives also. We have constructed 1,300 miles of telegraphs —the telegraph poles and wires all made in England; everything we wear, and almost everything ws consume, is imported from England. Can you tell me, then, that not a single unemployed workman in England is likely to secure a week's steady labour as the result of this enterprise? I can assure you it does them much more good than telling them about 'three acres and a cow,' because nothing has ever come out of that.

"With regard to the social programme of division, you know the old story. I think it was one of the Rothschilds who, having listened to this doctrine in a train, handed the gentleman, who had addressed him about it, a sovereign as his share of the plunder. We have to deal with this question, however, because we have to consider the feeling of the English people, who are most practical. You must show that it is to their benefit that these expansions are made, because the man in the street who is not a shareholder naturally asks, 'And where do I come in?' You must, therefore, show them that there is a distinct advantage to them in these developments abroad. That is the reason why, when we made a constitution for this country, I submitted a provision that the duty on British goods should not exceed the present Cape tariff, and I should like you to listen to me on that matter if I do not tire you. You must remember, as I have said, that your Little Englander very fairly says: 'What is the advantage of all these expansions, what is the advantage of our colonies? As soon as we give them self-government they do two things. If we in the slightest degree remonstrate with them as to a law they pass, they tell us they will haul down the flag, and they immediately proceed to devise how they shall keep our goods out.' The Little Englander says quite rightly that these people will not listen to any advice regarding administration, and as to manufactures they make every effort to bolster up bastard factories and to keep out our goods.

"It is very true that many of the Colonies have found out the folly of Protection, but they have created a bogey they cannot allay. These factories have been created, and workmen have gone out to them, and they are only kept going by high duties, and a poor minister who tries to pass a low tariff will have his windows broken by an infuriated mob. The only chance for a colony is to stop these ideas before they are created, and taking this new country of ours I thought it would be a wise thing to put in the constitution that the tariff should not exceed the present Cape tariff,

which is a revenue and not a Protective tariff.
The proof of that is that we have not a single
factory in the Cape Colony. I thought that if
we made that a part of our constitution we
should do two things—make a distinct tie
with England, and stop the creation of bastard
manufactories. You should be surprised that
that proposition was refused. But I will tell
you why it was refused : because it was not
understood. People thought it was a proposition for a preferential system ; in fact I may
tell you that all my letters of thanks came from
the Protectionists, and nothing came from the
Free Traders. It was, however, really a free
trade and not a protective proposition. A
proposal came from home that I should put in
words, to the effect that the duty on imported
goods should not exceed the present Cape
Tariff. I declined to do that, because I
thought that in the future—perhaps twenty-
five or fifty years hence—you might deal
with the United States as with a naughty
child, not altering the policy of England, but
saying, 'If you will keep up this McKinley
Tariff, we for a period shall keep out your
goods'; just the same as we go to war,

although we are not pleased with war. That is why I objected to the introduction of the words 'imported goods' and wished them to be 'British goods,' because England in future might adopt this policy, and yet have a clause in the constitution of one of her Colonies which prevented it. Who could object to this provision? Certainly not the French or German Ambassador, because, so long as England's policy is to make no difference, they come in under this clause, for the policy of England being that there should be no preferential rate, any law passed by us giving a preferential rate would be disallowed. This clause would have assisted German and French manufacturers so long as England's policy remained what it is, because they would also have shared in the privilege of the duty on British goods not exceeding 12 per cent.

" If you follow the idea, so long as England did not sanction a law making a difference, we had to make the tariff the same for all; but this great gain was obtained—that, supposing the Charter passed into self-government, and a wave of protection came over the territory, and they passed—say, a duty of 50 per cent.

on British goods, that law would be disallowed, because it was contrary to the constitution. The only objection that has ever been made to this proposition is that it would have been law as long as it was no good, and that when it was any good it would have been done away with. That shows the want of knowledge. People think that the Colonists are all for protection. Nothing of the kind. They know that with protection everything that you eat and wear costs you 50 per cent. more. But what does happen is that at times a wave of protection comes over a country, and it is carried by a small majority, the law is passed, the factories are created, and the human beings come out, and must be fed, and you cannot get rid of them. In the case, however, of a wave coming over a country under a constitution such as suggested, the Secretary of State would be justified in disallowing any such proposal. He would say, 'There is a large minority against it, and it is also against the constitution. I disallow it.' Look at the ramifications of it. If the gold is in the quantities we think it is in Matabeleland and Mashonaland that will become a valuable State of South Africa, and we know that there is going to be a Customs Union in Africa. This Clause being in our Charter would have governed the rest of Africa, and therefore you would have had Africa preserved to British goods as one of your markets. Take the comparison of this question, and I will show you what it means. There are sixty millions of your people in the United States. You created that Government; that is your production, if I may call it so. They adopted this folly of protection, and they cannot get rid of it now.

"What is your trade with the United States? Your exports there are about £40,000,000 per annum. In South Africa and Egypt we have only 600,000 whites, but your exports there amount to £20,000,000. You have £15,000,000 with the Cape and Natal, almost entirely British goods, and £4,000,000 with Egypt, where you have a fair chance for your goods. You are doing £20,000,000 with these two small Dependencies as against £40,000,000 with another creation of yours, which has shut your goods out, and where there are 60,000,000 of your own people. If they gave a fair chance to

your trade you would be doing £150,000,000
with the United States, to your advantage,
and the advantage of the American people.
I can see very clearly that the whole of your
politics should be to allow your trade to grow,
because you are not like France, producing
'grand wine,' and not like the United States,
a world by itself, but a small province doing
nothing but working up raw produce and dis-
tributing it all over the world. You have
done a wise thing, therefore, in remaining in
Egypt and in taking Uganda, and you have
to thank your present Prime Minister for
that. In one year that man has done this
against the feeling of almost his entire party,
which comprises the 'Little Englanders'—he
has taken Uganda and retained Egypt, and
the retention of Egypt means the retention of
an open market for your goods. The lesson is
so easy. Come to England. The last time I
came here I went on the Thames, with its endless factories. They were making goods—not
for England, but for the world. The other
day I went into a club, and saw four hundred
people standing about, and, for the sake of
amusement, I asked what they were doing. I

was told they were not doing business with
England, but with the world. There was not
a single man who was not doing something
with the world. The same thing applies to
everything here. It must be brought home to
you that—your trade is the world—and your
life is the world—and not England. That is
why you must deal with these questions of
expansion and retention in the world."

A speech of a totally different kind, wholly
unprepared and, in fact, a sort of familiar conversation, is the speech made at the banquet
given to Colonel Napier, at Bulawayo.
This is a specimen of what, for want of a
better term, I will call Mr. Rhodes's Veldt
speeches, which are made entirely on the
spur of the moment and which contain,
necessarily, a good deal of matter of merely
momentary or local interest. Addressing himself to the men of Rhodesia, he told them that
he had been a happy man since he came among
them. It was an old wish of his to live there

and guide the development of the country. In 1891 he told the Dutchmen of the Paarl "there will be no happier man than myself if you say the dual position is impossible to reach. I can then go and live with those young people who are developing these new territories." Here we follow him as he talks to those young people on the subjects that are the common interest of their lives.

This Veldt speech is also specially interesting as giving Mr. Rhodes's view of the prospects of Rhodesia, when fresh from his latest expeditions through it, put before the experienced residents of the country who composed his audience. I have omitted portions of the speech.

"Looking back on the war in Matabeleland, however sceptical any one of us may be, you will admit that out of 300 men who went out to fight the natives numbering about 6,000, the record of a butcher's bill of about 75 is a very fair one. After you had broken the natives up, we were fortunate enough to get Imperial troops and to have them under the guidance of General Carrington, and I think we should be thankful that when Her Majesty's Government thought it advisable to assist us, they sent us a man like General Carrington, the best part of whose life has been connected with the Colonial service. Some of you have considerable sympathy with myself. I may say that it is not needed. If you were to look at what is the pleasantest thing in life, I think you would find that the development of a country as big as France, Germany, and Spain combined is work that would be pleasant to anyone. You have been good enough to give my name to the country which you occupy. In viewing the various courses in life, which a man pursues, I cannot think of any pleasanter course than the development of a country in which the inhabitants have so firm a belief. When I viewed the country in the various commandoes, that I have been with, I found how good the country is. I find it is admirable for agriculture; it is without a rival in reference to stock, and I feel quite clear about the future even if the mineral development be not what you expect it to be. I repeat to you what I have repeatedly said to shareholders, the world has never met with a country which, being 400 miles in length and 200 miles in width and mineralised in every direction, does not contain paying properties. One satisfaction I feel over our present difficulties is that it is undoubtedly hastening your railway.

"I have told you plainly about the offer of Mr. Pauling to bring you the railway to Bulawayo by 1897, and they are pushing on the railway from Beira as hard as they can. The war, therefore, has not been an unmixed evil. You have the offer, which is almost concluded, of a railway by 1897, and we have given our pledge to Salisbury to unite you by speedy railway communication. Those who are here as representatives of companies and syndicates will be able to deal with their properties on a fair basis; whereas with meal at £7 or £8 a muid, and timber at such high prices, you would find it very difficult to work any mine and make it pay. And so I would put it to you that the war has not been an unmixed evil, for it will bring speedy railway communication, on which all your success must be based. As for myself you have been kind enough to ask me to speak, which I did not expect, but I may tell you in very plain language that in the circumstances in which I now find myself with you, and in so far as the judgment I have been able to form goes, you can have no pleasanter ideal than the work of developing a country from barbarism to civilization.

"I am amongst you, and you have done me the favour of giving this country my name. My return for that will be to make this country as great as I can. Please remember that I individually respect, and feel for any one who has had the feeling of adventure strong enough to come out of civilization and to take his risks of this country.

"Do not let us think for one moment that we are in a country of no prospects; we are in a country with every prospect. When you speak of the Government—it is natural to go for someone—remember the Government has had great difficulties which it has passed through, and so far as the thoughts of an un-official individual are of use, I repeat what I said the other day, that the first question is to get the railway to you and to get the war over, and I feel confident that if General Carrington remains with us we shall get it over soon. With the enormous mass of minerals that exist —I believe that 60,000 claims have already been pegged—I am perfectly certain that you will find any quantity of payable gold. And then when you get the rights of civilised citizens, I see the way to glide from the present position to representation for the people, and from that to a state of self-government by the people. You may say that a charter is ridiculous, but it is the first step. With the first step under the Imperial supervision, you would not have had the railway or the development, on account of the timidity of the English people; but I would be the first to say that it is only temporary, and that our government must be first by an elective system, and finally by a full and complete system. If you claim to be a politician you must think these things out, and what I said the other day, when you were good enough to give me a dinner, I repeat —amalgamation with the Cape would not be justice to this community, on account of the distance; but you can grow into a self-governing body. There are many of you here who

think that you will make your pile and dis-
appear. Now I am going to make a forecast.
I have seen the same thing in Kimberley and
in many parts of South Africa, and you will
find that when the pile is made you cannot
throw yourself back into English life, and you
will soon find yourself back again. The future
is big; it is fast bringing up the railway, and
then out of those endless minerals certain reefs
will pay, and we shall grow into a big community, and while we accept the present system
we will look at the future, which will bring us
a share in the government of the country. We
shall develop the State, not on lines of antagonism with the rest of South Africa, but in
harmony with it. We must be careful; we
cannot take responsibility at present; the temporary position suits us. With railway communication will come proper development and
proper working of the reefs that we possess.
As soon as that occurs and our population in-
creases we shall have the confidence to take the
responsibility of our position, and we shall
take that position not in antagonism to the rest
of the States in South Africa, but in perfect
harmony with them.

PERSONAL REMINISCENCES OF
MR. RHODES.

By DR. JAMESON.

.

PERSONAL REMINISCENCES OF MR. RHODES.

CHAPTER I.

I HAVE been asked by the author of what is practically the first biography of Cecil Rhodes, who, at any rate, knows his subject, though I have not read his book, to supply what reminiscences I can give of Mr. Rhodes. Having lived with Mr. Rhodes so many years, and being one of his oldest friends, I have much pleasure in doing my best, though I am no penman. The best part of twenty years has passed since I first met Mr. Rhodes. It was at Kimberley, in 1878. I had come out and settled there to practice as a doctor. From the day of my arrival at Kimberley, when I fell in with him, we drew closely together, and quickly became great friends.

Rhodes was then steadily working at his great scheme for the amalgamation of the diamond mines. He had been at work at it for years, and had still nearly ten years of persevering effort before him, for the amalgamation was not completed till 1888. We were young men together then, and naturally saw a great deal of each other. We shared a quiet little bachelor establishment together, walked and rode out together, shared our meals, exchanged our views on men and things, and discussed his big schemes, which even then filled me with admiration. I soon admitted to myself that for sheer natural power I had never met a man to come near Cecil Rhodes; and I still retain my early impressions of him, which have been fully justified by experience.

Even at that early period, Cecil Rhodes, then a man of twenty-six or twenty-seven, had mapped out, in his clear brain, his whole policy just as it has since been developed. He had obtained his opinions from no book, and no other man. He had thought out everything for himself independently; his success when he put thoughts into action increased his confidence in himself. He has good reason for his self-confidence. Where are you to find so large a man of ideas combined with so big a man of action? The rare amalgamation of these two kinds of men in Cecil Rhodes results in a statesman compared with whom a mere parliamentary leader in England, however consummate his skill, looks very small indeed.

I remember his first big speech at Cape Town. He was living with me at Kimberley, and was down with fever. He had not written a note, or a line of the speech. In fact, he had not put it into shape at all. He thought the subject out the night before he got up from his sick bed, and, though still very shaky, travelled down to Cape Town. This was in 1884. The speech was a big success. It was the first statement made in the Cape House as to his Northern Expansion policy, and shows the continuity of that policy. That policy consisted of the occupation of the *hinterland* of the Cape, by which he proposed to effect the ultimate federation of South Africa. He used to talk over all his plans and schemes with me, and, looking back at them now, it surprises me to note how little change there is in his policy. It is substantially the same to-day as it was then. He had, for instance, even at that early date (1878-9) formed the idea of doing a great work for the over-crowded British public at home, by opening up fresh markets for their manufactures. He was deeply impressed with a belief in the ultimate destiny of the Anglo-Saxon race. He dwelt repeatedly on the fact that their great want was new territory fit for the overflow population to settle in permanently, and thus provide markets for the wares of the old country—the workshop of the world.

This purpose of occupying the interior and ultimately federating South Africa was always before his eyes. The means to that end were the conciliation, the winning of the Cape Dutch support. They were the majority in the country, he used to say, and they must be worked with. 'I recognise the conditions and I shall make all the concessions necessary to win them. I mean to have the whole un-marked country north of the colony for Eng-land, and I know I can only get it and develope it through the Cape Colony—that is, at pre-sent, through the Dutch majority.' This idea of the occupation of unoccupied Africa, both South and Central, for England's benefit, was always in Cecil Rhodes's mind, from the time I knew him ; and how long before I cannot, of course, say. I only know he talked about it just as freely and frankly when I first knew him, and his schemes seemed all in the air, in

1878, as when they grew ripe for fulfilment ten years later, in 1888.

Next to his powerful mind, what most struck me in Cecil Rhodes was his independent attitude towards all questions that came up for discussion.

The speech which set forth his Northern policy, was the cause of the High Commissioner sending him to Bechuanaland, to deal with the Boer freebooters, in 1884. It had besides made his mark in the House. He was listened to, ever after, with attention. A thing I have noticed in Mr. Rhodes is the way he sticks to his ideas. The ideas he has in 1897 are the ideas he had in 1879, only he has, of course, matured them. In the same way his Northern policy to-day was his policy unknown then to any but intimate friends, eighteen years ago, before he had put up for a seat in the Legislative Assembly.

People talk of him as an opportunist. No doubt he is on matters he thinks unimportant.

On what seems important to him, he has always been absolutely independent. Take his relations to the Bond.

Sometime before he became Premier, when Sprigg's Ministry was in, Mr. Rhodes met Mr. Hofmeyr at a dinner. Mr. Hofmeyr thought Rhodes would be a more competent Premier than Sprigg, and offered him to come in as the nominee of the Bond. Rhodes refused. He was willing to work with the Bond, but refused to be their instrument.

It is perhaps not generally known that Mr. Rhodes has never joined the Bond. He was willing to lead them and to conciliate them, but he always kept his independence of action throughout. He wished to be fair to the Dutch, but the British was to be the governing race in South Africa, and the supreme flag the British flag. Mr. Hofmeyr, confident in himself, thought that he could manage and make use of Mr. Rhodes, but he has since found out he mistook his man.

Rhodes likes the Dutch individually : if he be asked to support their rights—Yes ; but if he be asked to support the Dutch as a governing body—No.   He has never changed from this attitude.

One of the facts that weighed with Mr. Rhodes in deciding to start the Chartered Company in order to occupy the Northern territories, was the fact that the Imperial Government, after they had spent about a million in Bechuanaland, had nothing to show—not a settler in the country — and progress and development not so much as attempted.   I dwelt on this point in a speech at Cape Town at the end of 1894, when I compared what the British Government had left undone in Bechuanaland with what the Chartered Company had done in Rhodesia.

Mr. Rhodes considered that he would have done something more had he had the management of a company with the same amount of money to spend ; and this he has practically proved in the general development of Rhodesia by the Chartered Company.

I have a very bad memory for stories, but here is one, characteristic of Mr. Rhodes's way of doing things, which is certainly never dull or commonplace. I was up at Victoria in 1893. The Matabele impis were close to the town, and kept attacking and killing our Mashona workmen. I remonstrated with them, and ordered them off in vain. I was besieged with complaints from the settlers, who threatened to trek out of the country if these marauders were not promptly brought to reason. I sent Lendy to drive them off, if they would not go quietly. They fired on him, and he charged and broke them, inflicting considerable loss. Thereupon other *impis* advanced and threatened Victoria.

Rhodes was down at the House at Cape Town. I wired to him from Victoria the exact situation, and said it was an absolute necessity to assume the offensive, and strike straight at Bulawayo at once. Rhodes, who does not waste words, wired back briefly, " Read Luke fourteen thirty-one." Of course, I had not a notion of what he meant.

This enigma could, no doubt, be made clear by reading the passage. I asked for a Bible and looked up the passage and read: " Or what king going to make war against another king, sitteth not down first and consulteth whether he be able with ten thousand to meet him that cometh against him with twenty thousand." Of course, I understood at once what Mr. Rhodes meant. The Matabele had an army of many thousands. I had nine hundred settlers available for action. Could I, after careful consideration, venture to face such unequal odds?

I decided at once in the affirmative, and immediately telegraphed back to Mr. Rhodes at Cape Town " All right. Have read Luke fourteen thirty-one." Five words from Mr.

Rhodes and eight from myself decided the question of our action in the first Matabele war. This story I give to show what a man of action and not of words Mr. Rhodes is.

The decision had its difficulties, besides the smallness of the number of men. Mr. Rhodes knew the Chartered Company's coffers were empty, and that if it was to be war he would have to find the money out of his own private purse.

Observe, too, Mr. Rhodes left the decision to the man on the spot, myself, who might be supposed to be the best judge of the conditions. This is Mr. Rhodes's way. It is a pleasure to work with a man of his immense ability, and it doubles the pleasure when you find that, in the execution of his plans, he leaves all to you; although no doubt in the last instance of the Transvaal business he has suffered for this system, still in the long run the system pays. As long as you reach the end he has in view he is not careful to lay

down the means or methods you are to employ.
He leaves a man to himself, and that is why
he gets the best work they are capable of out
of all his men.

I was forgetting one of Mr. Rhodes's most
prominent characteristics, which from the first
impressed me greatly.   This characteristic
is his great liking for, and sympathy with
the black men, the natives of the country.
He likes to be with them, he is fond of
them and trusts them, and they admire and
trust him.   He had thousands of natives
under him in the De Beers mines.   He carefully provided for their comfort, recreation
and health.   He was always looking after
their interests.   He liked to be with them,
and his favourite recreation every Sunday
afternoon was to go into the De Beers native
compound, where he had built them a fine
swimming bath, and throw in shillings for
natives to dive for.   He knew enough of their
languages to talk to them freely, and they

looked up to him—indeed, fairly worshipped the great white man.

It was just the same at a later date. He likes to have the natives round him, and be a sort of father to them. In his house near Cape Town there are no white men or women servants; his servants are all native boys, Matebele, Mashonas, and boys from Inhambane.

At the native school, near Groote Schuur, he has two of Lobengula's sons, who have the run of the house and garden at Groote Schuur on Saturdays and whenever they have a holiday. I have often watched them feeding in the strawberry beds and the vineries at Groote Schuur. They never go back to school without going to have a personal talk with Mr. Rhodes.

They, in common with all the other natives, delight in their big, kindly, white friend. Mr. Rhodes, though perhaps he is not a perfect master of their language, always makes a point of talking to the natives in their own tongue.

I have had opportunities of observing all this because I have lived a good deal with Mr. Rhodes at Groote Schuur on my visits to Cape Town. His trusted body servant for twenty years is a coloured man. Need I say that Mr. Rhodes is absolutely free from contempt for the black man. He looks upon him and treats him as a fellow man, differing simply in his lower level of development.

He is really, by nature, strangely and deeply in sympathy with the natives. He regards them as children, with something of pity in his affection for them, and he treats them like children, affectionately but firmly. It is for this reason that the success of his great Indaba in the Matopos was no surprise to me. Besides, I have been with him at many Indabas in former years in Mashonaland and Matabeleland. We went together right through Mashonaland in 1891, and again went about among the natives there in 1893 and 1894. He always got on wonderfully well with the natives. He likes and trusts them, and does not conceal his feelings, which they are quick to perceive. They like and trust him in return. I have never seen any one else who had the same sympathy with them. If there is a man in South Africa who deserves the title of the black man's friend, it is Cecil Rhodes.

IN his management of the Chartered Company's territory Mr. Rhodes was, of course, almost from the first, closely associated with myself, and I had continual opportunities of observing the methods of his supervision. I had already done a good deal of work in the country when I succeeded Mr. Colquhoun in his duties of Administrator in the end of 1891. From that date till the end of 1895 everything that Mr. Rhodes did in Rhodesia necessarily came under my observation.

He took the deepest interest in the work of developing the country, and made himself acquainted with everything of importance that occurred. He took care that the individual officials who represented him should be thoroughly acquainted with his views, and trusted them to carry out those views in his absence.

He did not, however, leave them to themselves for any length of time. He went up to the Chartered Company's territories at short intervals, and not only visited the towns but went through the whole country, making journeys in all directions in order to see for himself that his views were being carried out. He felt his responsibility as Managing Director not only to the Chartered Company's Board but also to the Shareholders, whose interests he did all he could to further. He also felt deeply his responsibility for the trust placed in him by the Imperial Government when they gave the Charter, and in the discharge of his duties as Managing Director, the consciousness of this twofold responsibility to the Company and to the Empire was continually present with him.

As regards extension and development his work speaks for itself. As regards the treatment of the natives, I may say a few words.

In introducing a civilized government into the country, the natives, Mr. Rhodes considered, could not be expected at once to understand the white man's civilized methods. Accordingly he desired that as far as it did not conflict with the safety of life and property, the natives should remain as much as possible under the native laws to which they were accustomed, administered through their chiefs, to whom their hereditary attitude was an absolutely feudal loyalty.

An important part of my work in Matabeleland in 1893 was to teach the native Indunas the change in the law, which was considered necessary in substituting the Chartered Company's rule for that of Lobengula. This change consisted mainly in the much more serious view we took of the prevalent crimes of rape, murder, and witchcraft leading to murder. On Mr. Rhodes's journeys through the country, following the conquest of Matabeleland, all the Indunas were summoned to meet him, and it was carefully explained to them in detail what the requirements of their new rulers would be. As far as possible the natives were to remain under their own tribal law; but the white man's laws for the protection of life and property, and also for the protection of the women from rape, were to be strictly enforced. Witchcraft, also, which led to murder, was to be severely punished.

This, of course, was also the method that had been carried out in Mashonaland, where the Chartered Company had been the rulers prior to their conquest of Matabeleland.

As regards the question whether or not crime was equally dealt with alike among whites and black men, one can safely appeal to the Magistrates' records of the cases tried in the various districts since the occupation of the country. The Magistrates' reports of their cases were all sent to, and carefully preserved

in, the Crown Prosecutor's office. The laws of
the Cape Colony were strictly enforced, and a
record of anything beyond the mere petty cases,
had, by law, to be sent to the Judge of the High
Court before the sentence was confirmed.

I fearlessly appeal to the clergymen and
missionaries of the various denominations in
the country, to the four London Missionary
Society missionaries, who had been years in
the country, to the four Roman Catholic
priests, to the four clergymen of the Church of
England, the three Wesleyan missionaries, and
the two clergymen of the Dutch Reformed
Church, as to any real case which could be
named, which the authorities have failed to
investigate, and deal with in accordance with
its merits, meting out the same equal justice
to black man and white.

The prison system and prison accommodation
in Rhodesia would compare favourably with
that of any country town in England. Black men
and white had exactly equal treatment in prison

as when on trial; but of course were kept separate, though in the same prison. The Magistrates were not allowed to use the lash, which could only be inflicted by order of the Judge of the High Court in very serious cases, as in the Cape Colony and in England.

The question of the land and cattle of the natives was dealt with practically by the Imperial Government not by the Chartered Company.

A Commission was appointed for the purpose, consisting of one Imperial Representative, Captain Lindsell, who was at that time Magistrate of the Tati district under the Imperial Government, one representative of the Chartered Company, approved by the Imperial Government, Captain Heyman, and the third member to act as Chairman of the Commission, Mr. Vincent, who was at the time Crown Prosecutor of British Bechuanaland, and who was appointed Judge by the Imperial Government, to take up his duties after serving on the Land and Cattle Commission.

The Imperial Government further provided that after the Land Commission was dissolved, its duties being finished as regards cattle and native locations, that the Judge himself should act on the Commission in case of any disputes subsequently arising on any of these subjects.

The general marking of the cattle was for the protection of the natives' cattle from the thefts of the low whites who came into the country, and from the thefts of the cattle-lifting Boers who came across the Limpopo from the northern Transvaal. The Boers of Zoutspanberg used to cross the river sometimes to lift cattle, sometimes to exchange the rifles they had been given by the Boer Government for Government cattle, knowing that they could always get a new rifle from Pretoria on the plea of having lost their own. This is the chief source of the supply of rifles and ammunition which the natives used in the recent Rebellion.

I have said enough, I think, to show to any

fair-minded enquirer that Mr. Rhodes cannot justly be charged with any neglect of duty in his management of Rhodesia, or with any harshness to the natives. At all events the most sceptical will be convinced if he will take the trouble to investigate my statements and thoroughly test their truth.

L. S. JAMESON.

PRINTED BY J. S. VIRTUE AND CO., LIMITED, CITY ROAD, LONDON.